THE FORTHRIGHT SAGA

BY

SUE MILLARD

Best wishes

Sue Millard

Dec 2012

Jackdaw E Books, 2012

THE FORTHRIGHT SAGA

First published in Great Britain 2012
ISBN 978-0-9573612-3-2

JACKDAW E BOOKS
Daw Bank
Greenholme
Tebay
Penrith
Cumbria
CA10 3TA
http://www.jackdawebooks.co.uk

Other books
from Jackdaw E Books in 2012
Coachman
Dragon Bait

THE FORTHRIGHT SAGA

Contents

1 :: Nora

Nora Forthright stepped heavily over her scrubbed-and-rudded doorstep and pulled the front door shut. She gave it a second tug to check the latch had engaged, then stumped off down the lane towards the Post Office.

The little town of Dangleby was as stout and uncompromising as Nora herself: grey stone terraces with squat chimneys spouting smoke that the wind rollicked away across the wet fields. If the rain kept off, the sheets on Nora's backyard line would soon be dry and she could press and air them before night.

She leaned into the Post Office door as though it were being held shut by a Force 9 gale, and a little brass bell tinkled in reponse.

"Mornin' David. Ow ista today?" Nora's voice had been honed by a lifelong battle with milking machines, tractors and sawbenches, and pitched for distance by the need to communicate with family across bare uplands; the voice of the Cumbrian farmer's wife. Though her widowhood had long separated her from the rented farm, the voice remained and it attacked the Post Office's plate-glass without mercy. David was as well-matured as Nora and knew from his own physical condition that she was probably a little deaf.

Giving his baritone a touch more timbre than usual, he said, "I'm very well, Mrs Forthright. You're looking in good fettle."

She picked a wire basket off the stack. "Oh aye, Ah's right enough. Have ye any taties?"

"There's a bag of Wilja just come in," he said. He relocked the cubbyhole after himself and directed her to the potato-sack in the corner of the vegetable display.

"Ah'll have ten pound," she said, and leaving him to attend to this she began to haul carrots out of the box and cast them ruthlessly into the basket. He averted his eyes from her upended brown tweed rump. Somehow he always expected its scent to involve a lurking undertone of silage and cow manure. In fact, although she did smell aggressively, it was of washing powder and deodorant soap.

"Cooking for the family this weekend?" he said, assessing the unusually large quantity of potatoes and carrots.

"Our Jonty's still settlin' in. Not that he was ever a great hand with a stewpan, even before he married her. This and a couple of pounds of shin ought ter feed him and Wayne for a night or two."

"You've no rush to catch the butcher's van," said David. "Aggie Tate says he's running late."

Nora grunted her thanks. The rest of the shopping followed her usual pattern: onions, leeks, one dessert apple (carefully selected), three cooking apples (random), a packet of cream crackers, one pack of butter and another of lard, a bag of self raising flour, a jar of jam (blackcurrant) and a copy of the *Messenger*. David, whose selling patter was nearly as unvarying as Nora's buying, enquired if she wanted any bread.

"Ah's baking tomorrow, so Ah's all right, thanks."

"Eggs?"

"Nay, our boy's fetching some from Bert's hens, thanks all the same."

"You don't want a lemon for your gin and tonic?"

Drawing herself up and adjusting her bust, she looked him squarely in the eye. "You know as well as Ah do, David Walker, Ah don't drink gin. The only call Ah have for a lemon is for a whisky toddy if Ah have a cold."

David acknowledged this regular rebuke with a cheerful, "Aye, well, you do right." He heaved the potatoes into a plastic carrier which bore the logo of a supermarket in Nether Goosethwaite (pronounced "Gusset"). Nora followed him as he hobbled towards the till, where she effortlessly lifted the potatoes into her canvas bag.

He expected her to reorganize the rest of his vegetable packing as she normally did, but today while he was totting-up the purchases, her fingers lingered on the weekly *Messenger*, and fluttered the edges of the pages.

"Have you had one of your letters printed, Mrs F?"

Nora's hand fell away from the newspaper at once. "Ah might have. Need to look t'be sure. Don't let me hold you back, now. What's t'damage?"

He told her the total, and she grunted and paid him.

"I shall have to go and get my reading glasses," he said, trying out a smile. But she hefted the groceries impatiently, so he hobbled round to open the door for her.

"I always enjoy your point of view," he said, and the little doorbell tinkled as if in agreement. "It's not every paper would print letters like yours."

"Aye well," said Nora, stepping solidly from the shop, "Common sense. Editor's a woman. Morning."

David closed the door, and waited until her moss-green beret had vanished round the corner before he picked a *Messenger* from the stack. He perched his bottom on the rickety bar-stool and his reading glasses halfway down his nose. Taking a buttermint from the jar under the counter, he unwrapped it, leaned back against the wall and sucked contentedly while he thumbed over the pages.

The *Letters* were addressed to the Editor, Mrs Hilary Tiverton-Dick.

~ ~

Dear Hilary Dizzily-Sick

My children, poor darlings, are always dreadfully ill when they travel in the back of my Handover Dispensary 4 wheel drive. My husband says it's the way I drive but I'm sure it's something more elemental, if you know what I mean?

I've heard that an earthing strap can help. Do any of your readers know where I can find a water diviner or dowser to point out the best position for it?

Too kind of you to help.

The Honourable Meriel Appleby-Station

~ ~

David had decided that Meriel was a trophy wife. It was being alone at The Grange all day that made her batty, of course – but then her husband was an oddity too. Richard Station was a collar-and-tie sort of bloke, tall, dark and strangely tough looking. You'd take him for a rugby man, rather than the cricket player that he was. It was two years since he had moved into Dangleby, and still nobody was quite sure what work he did. The two boys were away at prep school and seldom visited the shop, so David had little opportunity to make casual enquiries.

He sucked at his buttermint. The twist of his mouth and cheek might have indicated that he was exploring the upper reaches of his dental plate, but that was just camouflage in case a customer interrupted his enjoyment.

There was a letter from young Alan, too, who seemed to be staying up half the night chasing mythical animals.

~ ~

Dear Editor Person

I am doing a research project for my Not Very Qualified Level 3 in Wild Goose Chasing. I would like to know whether anyone in the Dangleby area has seen a boggart recently. For those not well up in nature lore, a boggart is a cross between a badger and a fox, with the nocturnal habits of both.

My method of stalking is to cycle around after 11 pm on Fridays and Saturdays and watch for them crossing the road in my headlamp. Unfortunately they are very elusive animals and I generally find I have captured a large loose ball of greasy paper with fragments of fried potato inside. Could you put me in touch with someone who knows a more efficient method?

Yours

Alan Eversoe-Slightly, NVQ 2 Wild Goose Chasing

~ ~

David found Alan hard to fathom. He knew the course Alan had actually completed was a gardening one through the Agricultural College at Upper Goosethwaite, and he was now working part time in the garden of The Grange. The NVQ business in his letter was entirely fanciful. Even when asked directly, he never revealed any information about Richard Station. This was disappointing, but understandable, since Alan's dedication to the animal and plant worlds seemed quite often to exclude any interest in people. In David's opinion Alan would be better off with a full time job, like in the Parks and Gardens for the Council, somewhere with other blokes who would tease him out of his stupid hairstyle, and keep his mind occupied with tabloid newspapers and laddish humour. On the other hand, he did have principles, which was more than David could say of a lot of Post Office customers.

Ah, here was Nora's offering.

~~~~~~~~~~~~~~~~~~~~~~~~~~~~~~~~

Now then, Hobnob

I hear tell that the woman that runs the Transport Department for the Government wants to let traffic use the motorway hard shoulder. I never heard anything so daft. If something breaks down, that lane's knackered, and how does the fire, police and ambulance get to an accident?

Most of the spots round here are on single track roads, and with the Government closing down Post Offices, there'll be nobody sensible for firemen to ask the way. They'll all have to use yon Stat Map thingie, Tin Tin or whatever it's called. That'll send them round by the motorway, and it'll be blocked, and we'll all be burned in our beds.

I reckon she's been at the metal polish again.

Yrs Grimly

Nora Forthright

~~~~~~~~~~~~~~~~~~~~~~~~~~~~~~~~

David shuffled his bottom on the bar stool and adjusted automatically to its drunken response. Nora's support for the traditional Post Office was heartening. Her mistrust of satellite navigation systems was the other side of the same coin, since both were consequences of a naturally Luddite cast of thought which had intensified since Nora's other half, Joss, had expired some fifteen years ago.

Having extracted the juice from this batch of letters, David carefully re-folded the Messenger and returned it to the counter for sale.

2 :: Zak and Wayne

A dark-haired fat boy and a thin ginger one crouched in the bottom of a beech hedge beside the garden wall of The Grange. It made a good base camp for war games outside in the lane, and piracy inside the garden.

"C'mon, Wayne," wheedled the fat boy. "That Mrs Station leaves the kitchen door open. When she goes out to nag the gardener, we could nip in, easy."

"Aw, Zak! She'd come in an' catch us."

"No she wouldn't," Zak said scornfully. "She's one of them twig women. She'd scream and run for help."

"Yeah, and she'd fetch him, that gardener."

Last summer, Captain Zak had urged various Pirate Crews over that wall in raids for raspberries, peas and ripening apples. The Crews had all been young, skinny and quick, and Ernie, who had been the gardener there for many years, was none of those things. Unfortunately when Ernie retired the situation changed. The new gardener was also skinny and quick and he worked far more hours than Zak thought was fair. The garden was dug and manured, the plants sprouted in pots and under cloches, the fruit trees were neatly pruned and the raspberry canes had been cleared of everything but their last summer's growth. Zak hugged his denimed knees among the slender buds of the hedge, and resigned himself to the fact that it wasn't yet worth sending his new Crew plundering.

His previous Pirate Crews had long since mutinied to play elsewhere, and the choice of accomplices was becoming limited. He'd picked Wayne mainly because he was a new boy to the school. Being ginger-haired Wayne was easy to ridicule, and he was skinny and quick all right, but he wasn't anywhere near as biddable as he should have been.

"Dun't be such a mardy-arse," said Zak. "It wouldn't hurt to have a look indoors. They're rich, ain't they? Look at that fancy lamp thing they put up. Dad says it must've cost a fortune." The copper and etched-glass lantern over the front door had been a talking point for a week. "There might be summat. Big cars, locked gates, stands to reason they'll have things we can nick."

Wayne wriggled. His Dad was Nora Forthright's son, Dangleby born and bred, so in the back of his mind, he could hear the tones that his Grannie Nora would use if she found out he'd been stealing. Not the words; he could never predict what she would actually say. While it seemed scrumping had been all right in her own childhood, she'd tut-tutted and frowned theatrically behind those silly old-fashioned glasses when he tried to top her stories with Zak's Pirate invasions at The Grange. As for stealing, real stealing from inside somebody's house – oh no, he knew the shrill voice she'd use and his Dad's hard hand that would follow, and he wasn't keen on risking either of them.

"That gardener can run faster'n me, so he'd catch you no trouble. And there's cameras."

"Them things don't work," said Zak, ignoring the slur on his running speed. "Me dad says they're just dummies. We could nip in after school. I bet they don't turn 'em on until it goes dark anyway."

Wayne frowned over this; something didn't quite make sense.

"Grannie Nora thinks they're real," he said. "I'd rather play Spiderman."

Spiderman was a simple game to see who could climb highest in the local trees. It was one of the few challenges where Wayne's slighter frame was likely to overcome Zak's bulk, so Zak ignored the suggestion.

"We should come at a weekend. We'd have plenty of time then."

Wayne sighed and abandoned Spiderman. "I'm not missin' footie practice on Sat'dy."

"Sunday then," said Zak, knowing that Wayne had never yet been chosen to play for the team.

"I got jobs to do for Grannie Nora on Sunday. And the gardener might be here."

"He won't be workin' Sunday," said Zak scornfully. "Just cos your Dad works Sundays, don't mean wussy Alan does."

"Well what about Mr Station? I bet he's home at a weekend. I'm not gettin' anywhere near him – not with a name like Slogger."

"That's only cos he plays cricket. You wouldn't know him. You weren't here last summer."

"Wi' that big black car, I bet he's a drug dealer," said Wayne, his voice rising in desperation. "That's why he's got all them cameras. I bet that gardener's a drug dealer too."

"Him? He's not a drug dealer, he wouldn't need to do gardening if he was. He's that skinny I bet he sniffs coke. Bet Slogger Station pays him in coke an' that's why he's always so wired."

This worldly wisdom fascinated and confused Wayne so much that curiosity overcame his fears. "You don't smell coke, dummy, you drink it. Or else it's that black stuff Grannie Nora puts in the stove to burn."

"You sniff it up your nose," said Zak.

"You do not."

"Do. Darren's big sister Jade says."

Wayne thought about it for a moment. "That's weird. You'd drown."

"It's not a drink, dummy. It's like a powder. Darren says it tastes funny. Jade told him she'd lock hers up if he tried it again."

"Does it taste like Space Dust?"

"Yeah," said Zak with certainty. "I suppose it fizzes more if you put it up your nose." After a moment he said, "I got 50p, let's ga down the Post Office and get some."

Wayne was glad to do anything other than burgling Slogger Station's house. Besides, spending Zak's pocket money was pretty well the only perk of being his Pirate Crew. They scrambled out of the hedge and set off down the road.

When they asked David Walker for Space Dust, it was obvious from their agitated get-it-and-let's-be-gone manner that something was up. But they couldn't come to much harm with the sweet sherbet powder, so he sold it to them and gave Zak his change. His parting 'Take care now!" was cut short by the tinkle of the shop-door bell as they scampered out into the dusk.

The trial wasn't a success. They sneezed and coughed and choked over a noseful of Space Dust and had to go back to the time honoured method of 'dabbing' a sugary layer with a spit-wet finger. On their way home, Zak said thoughtfully, "The clocks ga back soon. When t'lighter evenings come we could try it."

Wayne realised from the bullfrog look on Zak's face that he was set on getting inside The Grange, no matter what.

"I don't like it," said Wayne. Even to himself it sounded like a whine.

"Who's gonna know?"

"Me Mam would."

"Your Mam?" Zak looked at him. "Who's she? You don't even know what country she's in."

"Do!" said Wayne, sticking out his lower lip. "She hears about things. I know she does."

"Yeah? See if she can hear this then." Zak grabbed Wayne's nose and shoved him backwards against the wall. Pain burst through Wayne's head from front and back and met as a starburst in the middle. He sobbed and punched blindly at Zak's podgy chest.

Zak stepped back out of the hedge and sneered at him.

"Yer Dad's at the farm till dark and yer Mam's gone away. There's nobody waiting at home for ya. We're gonna look inside Slogger's house, one way or another."

Wayne wiped his nose on the back of his hand, and licked off the blood. It didn't taste nearly as good as Space Dust. He trailed in Zak's wake towards the terraces where they both lived.

3 :: Meriel

Meriel Appleby-Station teetered across her lawn, her bare ankles sticklike above unlaced leather brogues. Her faded-blonde looks had a harassed quality, as though she was forever trying to calculate how much she owed the cleaner or whether her husband would let her drive the car. She paused to inspect a clump of emerging daffodils, and removed a stray brown beech-leaf from among the buds before she swayed into action again towards the vegetable plot.

"Coo-ee. Alan."

Alan Eversoe-Slightly, the self-advertised holder of an NVQ 2 in Wild Goose Chasing, had tied back his dreadlocks and was forking a barrowful of muck from the heap by the garage. Jonty Forthright had unloaded it there the previous evening. When he departed, clumps of the muck had strayed along the drive after him as though yearning to be back in the farm midden, so that Meriel's husband Richard had come into the house in stockinged feet, holding out his defiled shoes like an accusation. Soothing Richard had taken most of the early evening and Meriel had carried a raging headache up to bed, yet had been unable to use it as an excuse.

She was grateful that Alan's first action this morning had been to render the drive pristine once more. Now she gazed hungrily at him tramping backwards and forwards over the ground that he had dug during the winter, tipping each barrowful and spreading it with such wonderful vigour.

Although he must have heard her brogues approaching, slap slap, squeak squeak along the weedless path, he dug and threw another forkful before straightening to face her.

"Yes, Mrs Station?"

"*Appleby*-Station," she corrected, gently. "You know it's the one thing...'

"Yes, missus, you said."

Meriel enjoyed gardening, since plants in general had a lower IQ than she did and flowers weren't inclined to argue. Alan was only supposed to manage the grass, the vegetable plot and the beech hedge. Unfortunately managing Alan was beyond Meriel's ability. He was rather a dear, but he kept hatching plans for her garden, and they were disturbing. He'd already suggested twice that the elderly orchard should be replaced with Japanese-style stones and gravel, and three times that the terrace should become a raised bed full of spiky plants.

Meriel didn't like confrontation, but in the case of the terrace, she had become stubborn. It was the only place where she felt sheltered enough to sunbathe, and she didn't want aggressive planting surrounding her on the few days in the year when the sun shone. But somehow Alan's proposals hovered around her like a mist, intimidating, persistent. She couldn't bring herself to ask her husband to deal with Alan. Richard expected her to be as strong as he was. When she failed, he was decisive, so he might dismiss Alan altogether, and that would leave her alone in the house from the time the cleaner left until early evening. It was better to make alternative suggestions to divert Alan's energy, but she could only think of one topic of mutual interest.

"Has, er, has Richard talked to you about the vegetables this year?"

"I haven't seen him at all, missus."

"Oh good. I mean, oh, hasn't he? Do you think we ought to sit down and plan what we're going to grow?" She smiled vaguely, and handed him the beech leaf. He dropped it into the barrow with the muck.

"Maybe," he said.

"I mean ... Ernie was very good with the flower garden but he never rotated the crops, you know, and we really don't want the brassieres on the same ground as last year and the year before, it's so risky .... Don't you think?" Sometimes she wasn't sure her choice of words was correct. It was best to check.

"Do you mean the cabbages and sprouts, missus?"

"Yes. Richard doesn't understand these things but you and I do, don't we?"

Her gloves moved in vague, appealing gestures. Alan was half her age and she couldn't explain to him why she needed his support on a decision that didn't even register in her husband's mind.

"Yes, missus."

"Well, erm – when you've spread that load," she fluttered, retreating already, "come in to the kitchen and we can talk it over with a nice cup of tea and a biscuit."

Alan drank neither tea nor coffee. She knew that, but the phrases came babbling out as though her mouth had a life of its own. She hesitated a moment longer, hoping for further conversation, but he only nodded and went back to his barrow, so she gathered her jacket around her and teetered away. Her brogues slapped an accompaniment as she retreated round the corner of the house and braced herself to share the kitchen with him.

4 :: Alan

Alan approached the kitchen door warily. Meriel wasn't in sight. Maybe she had changed her mind about discussing the brassicas. Nevertheless, he kicked off his boots on the step, parked them inside next to Meriel's brogues, and prowled round the kitchen in his thick cotton socks. A large gardening calendar hung on the wall below the clock. He curled a lip at the personalized image for the month, a bird nest-box with Meriel's name apparently carved into the front. More interesting were the scribbled appointments, *Lunch w Jennifer 11:30 Bulloughs. WI MTG 7:30 Memorial Hall. Robbie & Jamie Exeat*. The line associated with *Exeat* covered a weekend. He dried his hands, lifted the calendar page and saw *Exeat* repeated over another weekend in the following month. He memorised the dates.

He went to the sink and scrubbed his hands with a nailbrush and cold water, scorning the pump of scented soap. He was aware that his socks, though clean on that morning, had developed a whiff of the cowshed as well as the subtler one of hard-worked Wellington lining. Nothing to be done about that, though, except to avoid standing near the warmth of the Aga. The dishwasher throbbed under the worktop, and next to the Aga a timer shaped like a hamburger sat ticking, which reassured him that Meriel had no ulterior motive in calling him in – unless, perhaps, she expected to achieve it before the last fifteen minutes were up. He checked the dates on the calendar again.

Meriel came in, the clop of velvet mules on the tiles syncopating with their slap on the soles of her feet. He lowered the page without showing any embarrassment and said, "Nice calendar."

"Isn't it!" she said with pleasure. "It was a Christmas present. Richard bought it, but it was really the boys' idea. So clever, the way the photographs all have my name in them somewhere." She hovered closer to him. "Erm – tea?"

He shook his head, the dreadlocks flapping a solid denial.

"Coffee then. Milk?" She drifted away to the Aga, and slid the kettle onto the hotplate.

"No," he said. "Thank you."

"Fruit tea? Very delicious. Wouldn't you like some? You can put sugar in it if you like."

"Hot water," he said firmly.

"Oh," she said. "I'm really sorry. I completely forgot you're a vegetarian."

"Vegan," he corrected, pressing his lips together.

"So stupid of me, not to know the difference. You'll have to explain it to me." She moved towards him again and he stepped back and bruised his heel on the doorstop. "Could you eat a scone, do you think?"

When he didn't answer, she wandered back to the wall cupboard and took out two china mugs and a clingfilm-covered plate of scones.

"Are you like the Jewish people who need to know that food is Kosher before they can eat it? Would you like me to list the ingredients?"

He shook his head. He wondered whether he should rub his heel or whether that would give her yet another excuse to fuss over him. He chose to stand still. She filled both mugs with hot water, dropped a cranberry teabag into her own, and led the way to the round pine table under the window.

"Do come and sit down." She patted the cushion on the chair next to her.

He followed, trying not to limp, and sat at the opposite side of the table. The plate of scones joined a copy of the *Messenger* and the two lay like goalposts between him and Meriel while she released the cling film. She seemed nervous, biting her lip and glancing at him as though she were doing something vaguely naughty. He didn't offer to help.

She put down the resulting loose ball of film and patted it. "Sit."

He stared. She was certainly loopy.

"How long have you been a vegetarian, I mean a vegan?" she asked.

"Four years, three months and twenty-one days."

It was her turn to stare. "Fancy knowing to the day. You don't count the hours as well, do you?" She giggled.

"Of course. We were having Christmas dinner, so it was very memorable." It would be impossible to explain that transcendental moment to Meriel, so he said, "My decision that day melded feelings, perceptions and understandings that began in my childhood."

She tilted her head sympathetically and gazed at him before she said, "So tedious for you, having to read all the ingredients on packets and things."

"I don't use packet food," he said scornfully. "Have you seen all the things in it that our bodies aren't designed to assimilate?"

"Oh yes, you're right, no, of course not," she said, and reached for the ball of clingfilm, which she moulded anxiously into a tighter shape.

"Processed flour. Refined sugar. They're all poisons. Cow's milk contains blood and pus, did you know that?"

"Eww, no, really?"

He saw her fingers tighten round the ball and knew he'd got to her. He rammed the point home. "It's a biological and bacterial cocktail. Quite apart from the stress that dairying puts on the cows."

Her gaze flickered from his hair, which he knew looked strange, to his scrubbed hands and back to his eyes.

"You're so earnest about your religion," she said. "Well, I know it isn't a religion, but it seems like it – the way you speak – you know?"

He was rather surprised that she mentioned religion. He had observed Meriel's churchgoing habit quite closely, and assumed that it followed the Dangleby tradition – saying Amen and singing obediently over a hymn book, and assessing other women's clothes in between times. He noticed that she had kneaded the clingfilm into a little sausage. Dismissing the possible meaning of this, he said, "We should eat food that's grown in tune with the moon and the sun. Fresh local foods are the only ethical way to health."

"That's why Richard and I decided we wanted a house with a nice large garden," she said, with a sigh that seemed unnecessarily breathy. "You know, Ernie was awful, he used pesticides – and some of them had been banned for years. Said he had a lot of old stuff..."

"I suppose he said he *might as well use it up.*"

"He did! Isn't that dreadful? Well, I couldn't have that. I wanted our garden to be *completely* orgasmic. I told you that at the interview, didn't I?" Her hand fluttered over her hair, settled down on the tablecloth, moved towards him, took a scone from the plate, retreated again. "Won't you have one?"

"No thanks. Now then," he said, "the brassicas. The cabbages were at the far end last year and the sprouts next to them..."

"Yes, so we should really move them this year." She took a small mouthful of scone and gazed at him.

"We could plant it properly as a four-year rotation," he said, and avoided her eye by marching his hands into the corners of a square on the tablecloth. "I'll draw up a plan."

"Oh yes," she breathed, and pressed a stray crumb into her mouth. "Every bed could be used in turn."

"Plot," he corrected her. He took a slurp of water, which was still far too hot. He didn't dare spit it out so he swallowed it and masked the pain as best he could.

"Of course. I want your advice about the caterpillars this year, too. I'm sure you have lots of better ideas than Ernie. We had such a fight over pesticides that he wouldn't use any prevention at all, especially not orgasmic methods, and the cabbages were just like lace. I don't know how you stop them. I spent such a lot of time last year picking off the caterpillars and squashing them. And clapping the butterflies. I hadn't realised they reproduced at such a terrible rate."

"You mustn't do that," he said as he recovered from the afterburn of the hot water. "We'll find a more humane method. I'll look it up."

"And when you draw up the plans for the garden, don't try to include that wet corner. If ever there was a place to plant rice in, that's it!"

"Ricin?" he mouthed, his mind galloping in four different directions.

She made a tent of the newspaper and held it over her head like a Coolie hat, and gave a nervous, whinnying laugh. "We really must do something about the drainage there."

He gulped at his hot water again. Her attempts at humour merely confused him.

She stopped laughing. "That reminds me," she said, "I meant to ask you about straps."

"Straps?" he choked.

"Yes, I wrote to the *Messenger* about the boys being car-sick in the Dispensary." And she patted the paper on the table.

"The – oh, the Discovery."

"Yes – my mind works in such silly ways, I just remembered you wrote a letter, didn't you, about nuggets..."

"Nuggets?" He tried to look serious and intelligent and as though he understood what on earth she was talking about. What had he written to the *Messenger* recently? "Oh – you mean boggarts."

"And I wrote a letter too. You see," she explained, turning the paper towards him, "here they are, side by side like two good friends. I hope we *are* good friends. I think this must explain why I saw you crawling through the garden one night last week."

"Did you?" He was scarlet now and sweating.

"Yes. I did think at first you were testing the ground temperature for sowing the salad crops, but it's too early in the season isn't it, and anyway one has to do it – er – without the trousers on, isn't that right?" She giggled again. "But you still had your trousers on so I knew it wasn't that and I was terribly puzzled. You must have been watching for nuggets, I mean boggarts. I wrote to the paper about that, too. I mean, I didn't know whether they might be dangerous. Perhaps I should get a dog, for protection?"

"No! No," he said urgently, "no, you shouldn't get a dog, that would be animal exploitation. You don't keep any prisoner animals. It's one of the reasons I'm willing to work here. Don't start now."

"You see?" she breathed, gazing at him with her washed-out blue eyes. "You have such an elementary background."

"I do?"

"Yes, I felt it the moment I met you. I can't think why I didn't think of asking you before. You know such a lot about boggarts, you're bound to know someone who can fit an earthing strap to the Disp – er – Discovery."

Alan nodded, meeting her gaze but not really conscious of doing so, as certain of his thoughts came together.

The timer on the worktop clicked and shrilled, and they both jumped. Meriel got up to open the top Aga oven, and a sickening waft of casseroled beef and sponge cake hit him in the chest. He stood up too, holding his breath until he had put on his Wellingtons.

"I'll draw up – an outline – of the plot for you," he said. "And I do know someone who could fit an earthing strap. You'll have to overlook his attitude – he's a bit of a rough diamond – but he's really in touch with elemental forces. I'll ask him. See what he says."

"Too kind," she answered, her slim paws padded now by oven gloves. "I don't mind paying cash – you know? And that reminds me – do buy some lime for the brassieres. We don't want them to get clubfoot, do we?"

In the garden, he walked straight through the vegetable plot to the tool shed. Safe from the view of the cameras, he dug out his mobile phone. The first number he called went to voicemail, so he keyed in another.

"Bex, it's me." The phone made quacking noises and he held it away from his ear. "Yes, of course I will – Bex – Bex, shut up will you! Get a pen and mark our calendar." He gave her the dates of the two Exeat weekends. "Never mind why. I'll tell you tonight. Look, where's Jezza? Is he at the puppy farm? I wish he'd turn his phone on. If you see him, ask if he's still in touch with that ex-army bloke."

5 :: Wayne and Nora go Shopping

David Walker sat at the shop counter with a cup of tea, a ginger biscuit, and the *Messenger*. He turned the pages, skimming the standard discussions about a village by-pass, a report on last week's Women's Institute talk, and advance notices for the local agricultural shows. The Letters were far more interesting. In the last issue Aggie Tate and Mrs Appleby-Station had monopolised the columns, and the first letter in this one saw Nora responding gallantly:

~ ~

Now then, Hobnailed Terribly-Thick

Canst kindly tell yon lass that's bothered with a boggart in the garden not to fret. All she has to do is to put an old kettle by the door of the coal hole, with a packet of cup-a-soup and one of those camping stoves. That will keep it out of the house. Oh aye, and a flake of hay to pack its socks every night. Spring's coming and I reckon it will be away to the fell afore so long, like the sheep.

Till then, she can send her husband out for the coal. Reckon he needs the practice.

Yrs grimly

Nora Forthright

~ ~

Good old Nora, bless her, dumping a practical answer onto a ridiculous imaginary problem. David put down his cup of tea and was re-reading the letter with wry amusement when the shop bell tinkled and Nora herself stumped in, followed by her grandson, Wayne. David closed the Letters and removed his glasses to show polite attention to her as a customer, but he drank off his tea; if he left it until Nora had done her shopping, it would be stone cold.

"Now then, Mrs F, are you well?"

"Middlin' thanks," said Nora.

"I see ye've the grand-bairn with you today. Hello Wayne."

Wayne stared at him. "I'm nine. I'm not a bairn."

"Oh, I'm very sorry." He winked at Nora.

She said, "This la-al monster's been left wi' me all day and our manners are wearin' a bit thin. Watch yer tongue, young man." She elbowed Wayne. "Apologise to Mr Walker."

Wayne clearly had to think about that - and David didn't blame him, since he hadn't said anything untrue or rude - but she uttered a peremptory cough, and he mumbled, "Sorry."

"School holidays," said David sympathetically, to both of them.

"Aye, our Jonty's busy wi' lambing," said Nora, "an' there's some days his boss can't do wi' the lad getting in t'road." She seized a hand basket and shepherded Wayne to the dry goods section. David heard her chuntering in piercing tones about good-for-nothing townie wives who went off and left honest working men with bairns to mind. He thought better of making any remark. Wayne was usually a ginger streak that flew in at tea time, dived into the freezer for oven chips and ran for the door as soon as he'd paid. Today was the first occasion he'd been still enough to be studied, and David felt a pang of sympathy for the motherless boy in Nora's ferocious care.

When she came back to the counter for David to scan the bar codes from her goods, he asked Wayne, "Are you helping Grannie tomorrow as well?"

"No," said Nora sharply, "he's away to play with Isaac Tate, aren't ye, Wayne? Just mind you an' Zak behave y'selves, and don't eat so many sweeties ye can't manage yer tea."

She nodded grimly at Wayne. His mulish expression could have been provoked by Grannie Nora's warning, her disparagement of his mother, the idea of playing with Zak, or simply his day spent "behaving himself." David couldn't tell which.

"Good lad," he said, not knowing what else to offer.

"Well, Ah can't hang about. There's bakin' to do for t' talk tonight. Afternoon, David." The shop bell tinkled again as Nora stumped out with Wayne trailing behind.

6 :: Meriel starts a Hare

It was supper-and-chat time in the Memorial Hall after the talk, which had been about 'The Drug Problem in our Inner Cities' and Miss Agnes Tate and her handbag were following Meriel Appleby-Station round the tea trestle. Aggie knew nothing of cities, neither their inners nor their outers, except for six-monthly visits to the dentist and optician and a regular cycle of embarrassing encounters with the breast-cancer screening system. She was quite prepared to accept the word of the young policewoman speaker. And having accepted it she filed it away and forgot about it, in the quest for more local gossip.

The Honourable Meriel's title was a magnet for Aggie. When Meriel paused to put a slice of her own sponge cake on a paper plate, Aggie did likewise. The cake acquired, she continued to hover.

"Hullo!" she said, in what she hoped was a sprightly manner.

Meriel smiled a vague and encouraging smile and took a bite of sponge cake. In response, Aggie deposited her plate abruptly between the lettuce and the tomato salad, dug in her handbag and exhumed a tightly folded copy of the latest *Messenger*.

"Your letter really *spoke* to me," she said rapidly, as she turned the creased pages. Meriel stood patiently while her letter was read back to her in thin, nasal tones.

"It was wonderful how my letter in your columns produced such a flood of advice for placing an earthing strap on my Handover Dispensary 4 WD."

Aggie stumbled a little over '4 WD' but Meriel gently contributed "four wheel drive" and she carried on:

"A friend has now put me on to a dowser in Pullet St Mary, who was able to install one for me."

"I didn't realise there *was* such a person," said Aggie, with an accusing look at Meriel. "My grandfather really could locate water. He dug wells for a living. He must have walked the length and breadth of the county in the course of his business."

"Mr Eversoe-Slightly," said Meriel, and she shivered a little at the use of his name, "was most helpful in directing me to the dowser chappie. We met in a mutually convenient place. Possibly he lived somewhere else. I didn't *ask*, of course."

"I'm afraid very few people have a genuine talent," said Aggie. "Most of them are frauds." She resumed:

"*I really think now that when my darling children are home on exeat from St Gullible's Preparatory School, they will find their travel sickness is no more. The fee was MOST reasonable –*

"I certainly hope it was," said Aggie. "Never mind. I suppose it's a mother's duty to do what she can. And at least your two boys are well behaved and polite."

"Thank you," said Meriel vaguely, her sponge cake poised at ear level, the paper plate neatly centred below. "Robbie and Jamie have quite nice manners, I think."

"Not like those horrid children from the terraces," said Aggie.

"Oh dear no. Between you and me, Alan has chased one particular boy away from our garden more than once. His friends keep climbing over the wall."

Aggie saw Nora, behind Meriel's back, reaching for a slice of chocolate cake. The hand paused momentarily, but Nora's conversation with the Methodist minister's wife never faltered.

"Your husband must get so frustrated," said Aggie to Meriel. "Having to spend his time dealing with trespassers, I mean." He was so dark, she thought; so tall, so seldom seen despite two years of living in Dangleby; so suavely enigmatic, like Rochester, or Darcy.

Meriel said gently, "Alan is the gardener. My husband is called Richard."

"Oh silly me – of course I knew that. What is it your husband does, again?" The lack of this knowledge was a constant irritant to Aggie's mind.

"He's a toxicologist," said Meriel, and having managed the word successfully she plunged onward. "He works between several labradors, you know. Always on the go. Such a busy life. We're lucky we see him at all."

Aggie nodded sympathetically. She had spent last summer helping with cricket club teas with the sole purpose of seeing Richard Station. Stiffening her thin back, she rattled the *Messenger* and returned to Meriel's letter. She struggled for several moments but seemed quite unable to read the next paragraphs aloud, and merely patted the newspaper with a frantic paw.

"*Now, darling H, as a thank-you I am sending you a CD of a group called The Bone Noses. On hearing it you will realise what a phenomenal talent you have hidden away behind your word processor. You could sing and play the guitar as well as they do when you had had only 2 lessons. Just think, you could give up the day job and become a Rock Star! Shall we contact their recording company or find a local one? Isn't it too exciting!"*

"Oh Mrs Appleby-Station, I can't believe you are encouraging rock music. You really mustn't. Our dear Hilary..." She lowered her voice a little, as Hilary was only a few steps away, noting down something that the young policewoman was telling her. "She does such a wonderful job in spite of the ridiculous decisions she has to report from the Council. Please don't suggest that she should throw it all away for a life of false glamour."

Meriel brushed crumbs from her finger tips, and tilted her head sideways as though considering this plea. "Do you think she might?" she enquired mildly. "Such fun."

"I don't know. I do, *do* hope not. It's so important that the organ of our community is managed by a feminine hand." Aggie rattled the *Messenger* again in a somewhat threatening fashion. "I really feel strongly on this. I hope you don't mind me saying so. It's very, very important."

"Not at all," said Meriel, her gaze drifting round the chatting ladies.

Aggie re-folded the paper and pushed it into her bag. "Well, it's been lovely talking to you but I think I ought to go now. I'm feeling rather flushed. It must be time for my medication."

"So nice to see you," murmured Meriel.

Aggie shuddered. "Next thing you know, dear Hilary will be abandoning the *Messenger* to run a drama weekend. Or even – even a festival! Don't encourage her." She scooped up her plate of cake, and hurried towards the exit.

7 :: The Raid on the Grange

Zak was in a rage because Mrs Tate was attempting to chase him outdoors for the day.

"Go out with Wayne," she said nervously. "Make the most of the sunshine."

"No. I want to play Dino Den."

"Not today, darling."

"Go to work! Go and leave us alone!"

"I've taken time off specially to spring clean your bedroom, darling. I'd like you out of it, just this once."

"I don't want you to spring clean. I want to play Dino Den."

"Take Wayne for a nice walk."

"No. I want to beat him at Dino Den."

Mrs Tate offered Zak a plastic box the size of a shipping container. "There's lots of nice sandwiches so you can share them with Wayne."

Zak slapped it out of her hands. "I want to play Dino Den!"

His mother flinched almost as much as Wayne did.

"Oh for heaven's sake," she babbled, "don't be such a baby. It's lovely weather. Do something constructive, play on the swings, ride your bike, have a picnic." She hurried away upstairs.

Seeing Zak turn red in the face, Wayne ran out into the street and sat on the wall. A window opened upstairs and he could hear Mrs Tate tra-la-la-ing and see the winter curtains twitching and collapsing out of view. He supposed Zak would stamp his feet and kick the sandwiches round the kitchen, but he wouldn't kick them so hard he couldn't eat them later, so he'd come out eventually because he couldn't concentrate on the Playstation while his mum was vacuuming and singing so loudly.

Wayne had ten minutes in which to ponder the mysteries of mothers (and grannies) doing spring cleaning before Zak waddled down the garden path. He had stuffed the huge lunchbox into a shoulder bag but he was still too cross to talk, so for lack of spoken direction they drifted towards the farm where Wayne's Dad was working.

Bert Askew was lifting a hay bale into the tractor transport box and gave them a stern look as they passed, so Wayne didn't hang about, but led Zak through a gate onto the field footpath. They heard the tractor start and rumble away. Confident that Bert couldn't see him, Wayne ran in wide circles over the pasture. His delight in the brisk air was too great to be spoiled by Zak sulking. He ran and jumped, and startled the lambs and dodged their mothers, and felt on top of the world.

Jonty Forthright came out of the lambing shed with a lamb dangling by its forelegs from each hand and the ewe trotting, whickering, behind. He walked well out into the field before he laid the lambs down, and while he waited for the ewe to come and claim them, he surveyed the rest of the flock. The nervous ripple of movement in the nursery field attracted his attention. He followed it back to its origin, identified the boys – the thin one running and leaping, the fat one trudging – and muttered, "Little buggers." But he waited till the ewe had tucked her lambs under her to feed before he ran up the field and bellowed at his son, "Git out o' that! Git back on the footpath!"

Wayne knew the ground far better than Zak. He made for the stile in the stone wall where the footpath led round the far side of the village.

"We'll be all right once we're through 'ere," he said to Zak as he climbed over. It was a different farm and out of his Dad's reach.

Wayne knew he'd have to wait for Zak to squeeze in and out of the gap in the wall, so he perched on a through-stone on the other side, and enjoyed the sunshine. A kestrel hovered and tilted on the breeze and Wayne sat still, trying to see what the bird was hunting.

"This is boring," grumbled Zak, as he struggled through. He dumped the shoulder bag and scowled at the field. The kestrel swooped away to prospect another slope.

When he got his breath back Zak said, "I should-a fetched the X-box. We could hook it up to yer Grannie's telly. You could carry it all right. C'mon, let's go and get it."

"Grannie won't let you," said Wayne. He had his own Nintendo, it was true – Nora had given him a second-hand machine for Christmas – but it had come from the Tates via Zak's Great Aunt Aggie, and was deeply scorned by Zak as something he had once discarded. Wayne knew very well that his playing skill was inferior to Zak's. With the extra speed of Zak's new console, the different interface designs and the fresh technical challenges, Wayne's avatar seldom managed to survive more than a few exchanges of play.

What Wayne's real body wanted to do was to run and climb trees and hang backwards off the playground roundabout, jump off the slide to land like a paratrooper in the tanbark, and roll down grassy banks until he was so dizzy he could only lie and laugh helplessly. "We'll have to think of summat else."

Zak heaved himself upright and said, "Time to see what's inside Slogger Station's house."

***

They knew the solid wooden gates of The Grange had an electronic lock, so they followed the wall until they reached the gap in the hedge.

Zak said, "I got a good feeling about this, hahaarr," and pulled a horrible face. "Get up an' have a look. See if anyone's about."

Wayne obediently vaulted halfway over the wall and hung there looking into the garden.

"The cars are out," he reported. "No gardener."

"What you mean by out? You mean you can see 'em on the drive, or they're not there?"

The coping-stones were pressing into Wayne's stomach and cut his breath. "Not there. The garridge doors are open. Might be one in there, can't see."

"Front door?"

"Dunno. Kitchen's shut though."

"They've gone out. Let's go and see what we can find."

Wayne sighed, swung a leg up and dropped over the wall, and waited behind a flowering bush that smelled of cats. There was a lot of scuffling and grunting before Zak found footholds on the beech hedge that enabled him to climb over and thump down beside him.

"There's a bedroom window open. I can see that from here. Hahaarr me hearties, I smell plunderrr."

Wayne was unwilling to venture onto the open lawn with the house windows all staring at him. "Never mind plunder – where've you left the sarnies?"

"They're in the hedge."

"I'm hungry. C'mon, let's have a sarnie. You'd like summat to eat, wouldn't you? I don't want to go in there."

"If we got to run for it, I can't climb with a lunchbox under me arm." Zak was checking for movement inside the house. "We can pick it up on the way back over."

Satisfied that there was no-one watching, he slouched over the grass and along the flagged path that ran under all the ground floor windows. He peered in at smooth plain carpets, pale furniture, and large, abstract pictures centred singly on the walls, while Wayne stared at neatly-knotted daffodil clumps in the lawn, and a roll of netting stretched along a row of young peas. Then he thought about the farm, where growing things were less tidied up, and he wondered if he preferred them that way.

"Where's the telly?" muttered Zak.

"You ain't gonna nick a telly!" said Wayne, shocked.

Zak shook his head. "We couldn't get it over the wall. DVDs, though, they'd be easy. Only I can't see any. They must have got the telly built into a cupboard or something. Posh people do that."

"Oh," said Wayne, and followed him round the corner.

The next room was tightly lined with bookshelves, all full, with more books stacked on the desk and tucked flat into crevices of the shelves. There was no clutter in the kitchen, and no food to be seen.

They completed a fruitless circuit of the house. Everything was shut and locked, even the French windows that Zak had hoped would let him through with no physical effort. The only thing that was open was the bedroom window. He struck a pose, pointing upwards.

"Cabin boy! Shin up that rigging to the crow's nest."

"What rigging? We've got no rigging."

"There's bound to be a ladder somewhere. How about the garridge? Go an' look."

"Why me?"

"Cos I'm Captain Blackbeard and you're the Pirate Crew." He stood, hands on hips, head back, a Sumo wrestler in baggy denim. "Get on, man, let's see what's in there."

Wayne licked his lips. "Me Dad would belt me."

"He isn't gonna know, dummy, if you don't tell him."

"And Grannie Nora would tell me off."

"So let her. She's gotta find out first."

Wayne desperately played his last card. "Me Mam wouldn't like it."

"Your Mam's not here, dummy. Stop whingeing on!" Zak stamped his feet on the path. "Get into the garridge and find a ladder!"

Wayne trailed across the garden, head down. He didn't mind being called "dummy." He didn't even mind Zak organising their day. But he did mind Zak reminding him that his Mum had gone away and wasn't coming back. He stepped inside the garage, and sniffed and blinked and wiped his face with his sleeve.

The big Discovery had been reversed in with its left hand wing mirror nearly touching the wall, so that the driver had room to get out on the right. There was an aluminium ladder hanging on brackets just beyond it but even Wayne couldn't squeeze through a space that small. He decided with relief that there was no way to lift the ladder down.

Then he heard tyres on the road outside.

For a moment he dismissed them as simply passing traffic, but they stopped and the garden gate-lock clicked. The gates crunched and clunked and began to open, revealing the Mercedes purring outside, ready to drive in. It was full of the Station family; Meriel in the passenger seat, two dark-haired boys seen dimly in the back. Slogger Station raised his hand off the remote control and pointed at Zak, and the emotions on his face were far more frightening than Zak's earlier tantrum. When Slogger began to open the driver's door, Wayne bolted unseen into rear of the garage and dived under the Discovery.

For a boy who didn't practise running Zak made a respectable start. He headed for the gap in the hedge with the accuracy of a rabbit for its burrow. But vaulting wasn't high on his list of abilities, and he was only halfway over the wall when Richard Station and his son's cricket bat caught up with him. His accurate swing whacked Zak's bottom with all the power of righteous anger.

Wayne, crouched behind a broad Discovery tyre, heard Zak's howl and stuffed his fist into his mouth. He wanted to giggle hysterically. In spite of the pounding adrenalin, he found he relished the sound of Zak's punishment. It fitted the sense of justice that Grannie Nora and his Dad had knocked into him.

The doors of the Merc opened and shut. "Mummy, who's that boy? Why's Daddy smacking him?" The voice was light, concerned, and exquisitely well spoken. Nice-but-dim.

Wayne shrank back a bit more. He was a long way from the garage doors, and that was both good because they weren't likely to see him, and bad because if they did, there was no escape.

"It's only Mrs Tate's little boy, dear," said Meriel, her voice muffled by reaching into the Merc for her bags. The older boy's snicker of laughter was swallowed by another howl from Zak. "Will you carry this for me, my darling? There's a good boy. Let's go inside in case Daddy wants us to call a policeman, shall we?"

Now maybe Zak would stop fretting to come in here!

"Mummy, won't the policeman tell Daddy off for hitting that boy?" The clop clop of Meriel's leather shoes moved away, followed by the boys' trainers squeaking over the gravel. Trainers with designer logos. Posh and expensive.

"It's only your cricket bat. It won't leave a mark," said Meriel's cool voice. "Come along." A wail, a crash and a rustle of leaves announced Zak's descent into the hedge on the other side of the wall.

"Don't let me catch you here again, fat arse!" shouted Richard.

Wayne stayed still, listening to the sounds of Zak scrambling away and dragging the lunchbox with him. After a few moments he heard Richard Station laughing.

Richard came back to the Merc, got in, drove it round to the garage, and got out and slammed the door. When he came towards the Discovery Wayne became a thin strip of terror, and slid completely underneath the car. But Richard only stood the cricket bat in a corner, and went back to the Merc for the remote control. Once the gates had crunched and shifted shut, he strode to the kitchen door and vanished inside.

Wayne peeled himself off the tyre, assured himself that his scuffed knees and elbows still worked, and considered what he ought to do. If the Stations remained in the kitchen, he could easily sprint to the gap and be over the wall before they saw him; but he couldn't check the house from under the Discovery. He eased himself out from under the car past the earthing strap, and as he did so, something fell to the floor behind him and made him jump. He looked out at the house. There were no faces at the windows. He glanced back at the something: it was cylindrical, like a can of furniture polish, and trailing a loose electrical wire. Had he knocked it off? He wasn't sure. He didn't think it had been there when he scrambled under the car, but perhaps he'd been in too much of a hurry to notice. Anyway, if a vehicle was under cover, it was there to be mended, so a loose wire was nothing odd, was it?

He peered at the house again. Nobody appeared at the windows. Nobody shouted. He took a deep breath, sprinted for the wall and was gone.

8 :: The Editor and the Women's Institute

Colleen Grace, local author of "Travels with a Doll," had been booked to speak to the Women's Institute since November the previous year, but her agent telephoned the Secretary two days before the meeting to give apologies. Colleen had had a car accident.

The Secretary sighed, and thanked her, and offered her best wishes for Colleen's recovery. Then she muttered a brief curse on defaulting speakers and went outside for a walk round the garden. She muttered, "Damn greenfly!" as she wiped them off the budding roses; "Opportunist!" as she pulled out a clump of grass; "Hooligan!" as she uprooted a dandelion and left it to shrivel on the path. That done, she straightened her back and admitted that her tulips were magnificent this year: a blaze of pinks and reds against the white rhododendron. The clematis rippled serenely over the stump of the apple tree and the saxifrages erupted from their stone trough into a cloud of creamy blossoms. As she surveyed them all, peace returned to her, and with it, her sense of humour.

After that, she did what she always did on such occasions. She crossed the road and tapped on the window of Hilary Tiverton-Dick, the Editor of *The Dangleby and Pullet St Mary Messenger.*

Hilary, though irritated by editing the last two weeks' letters, had recognised signs of trouble in the Secretary's gardening behaviour, so she lifted her glasses onto her hair, opened the window and leaned out.

"Hello Avis," she said. "What's up?"

"Urgent but minor, I hope," said Avis, threading her way carefully past the rambling rose. "No speaker for Thursday night. She's had surgery for a complicated fracture of her jawbone."

"That's a bit extreme," said Hilary, "couldn't she find a better excuse? Mind you," she added, "anaesthesia is just about the only thing that would shut Colleen up."

"You are awful," said Avis. "I'd have liked to ask her *why* – oh well, not to worry. The thing is, Hil..."

"You need a stand-in."

"Yes. There's only so many times we can invite Ernie Hodgson to discuss the power of snails to migrate back into the same garden you threw them out of. It's a question of sanity."

Hilary nodded. "Leave it to me."

***

Mrs Dobson, at the small Memorial Hall piano, led a very average rendition of "Jerusalem." When it was over and everyone had seated themselves, Hilary walked forward to the Secretary's table to face the rest of the assembled ladies. If she had paused to study her audience she might have trembled at the sheer mass of woman power, spread over the rows of chairs in its medley of shapes, ages, colours and patterns; but Hilary was one of them herself. She was their sister, and their voice as the Editor of the *Messenger*. She drew her glasses off her hair and perched them on her nose.

"Good evening," she said. "Now I know I'm no substitute for Colleen Grace, but don't worry, I'm not going to give a talk or anything of that sort. I would like to open a discussion. I'll keep it short and sweet and you'll be among the tea and cake a lot sooner than you would if Colleen had managed to get here."

Subdued chuckles.

"So – I'm standing here now to ask you all to join a new venture. The Reading Group and the Scribblers have already chosen to support it." Hilary glanced at the secretaries of those bodies, who nodded back to her. She unfolded a small poster for everyone to look at. "The Dangleby and Pullet St Mary Literary, Music, Dance and Drama Festival."

"That will be nice," said Meriel Appleby-Station, with an automatic smile.

Aggie Tate gave a little groan. "I knew it."

Nora shuffled herself back in the stackable plastic chair and stopped listening. She had complete faith in Hilary Tiverton-Dick's ability to organise such an event, but no ambition to take part.

"Our guest speakers will include three published writers," said Hilary, and she read their names off the poster; Colleen Grace was not included. "We will also have the chance to experience works by the owner of Studio Music, a choreographer from Manchester, the Poet in Residence from the superstore in Nether Gusset, and the choirmaster of Pullet St Mary."

The ladies leaned towards their neighbours, or twisted round to consult others behind them or in front, and most of them nodded.

"Some of you with children will know already that the primary and secondary schools have been invited to give musical, dramatic or literary performances. We will have open sessions and tasters where everyone can try a new art form." Hilary paused. "Right, that's my bit done. Over to you now – I'm sure you'll have questions."

There was an embarrassed silence. Avis coughed and was about to speak when Mrs Dobson raised a hand.

"Could we write and sing our own version of Jerusalem?" she suggested. "I've often wanted to transpose it into a different key."

This sparked a brisk discussion of the hymn book in current use at Pullet St Mary, leading to a consensus that most of the hymns were set too high.

"Thank you, ladies, thank you," said Hilary. "That's a start. I know some of you will already be involved in writing a play with the Scribblers, but are there any other suggestions? Does anybody want to lead a line dancing session?"

"My daughter goes to circle dancing. She might know someone."

With these ideas circulating, the conversation became general, and several ladies offered to run stalls, including a book exchange, a craft session for children to make bookmarks, and calligraphy where they could use specialist pens to write-out birthday card greetings and verses. Hilary made notes on the back of her poster and checked them with Avis.

Meriel stood up and asked, "Will there be any scope for gardening? Flower arranging sessions perhaps?"

Hilary was struck speechless. Avis came to her assistance. "I think gardening is adequately represented by the Agricultural and Flower shows, and the Harvest Festival, don't you? The Literary Festival is intended to enlarge our experience of other arts – correct me if I'm wrong, Hilary."

Hilary recovered her voice and said, "Yes. Yes, quite, thank you Avis," and Meriel sat down meekly.

At the end of half an hour, the only lady with any doubts seemed to be Aggie Tate.

"Will this event follow similar lines to the May Day Carnival?" she asked. Without waiting for a reply she plunged on, "If so, I really must protest. Wearing next to nothing does not constitute a fancy dress costume. In my day you covered everything up with crepe paper!"

"Including piano legs," muttered Avis to Hilary.

Hilary kicked her under the table and muttered back, straight faced, "Even she isn't that old."

"I've seen young people in Market Street," went on Aggie, over a rustle and a sigh of disagreement from the rest of the ladies, "with things on show that I didn't know anyone possessed. I watched all day and there wasn't one with a vestige of modesty. It was perfectly fasc – I mean, sickening."

"It wasn't at all," said one of the younger ladies robustly, and a few others murmured, "Hear, hear."

Meriel raised her gentle voice to ask, "But Miss Tate, why didn't you simply go indoors and watch television? There must have been a Consternation Street special that would have pleased you better."

"It was my duty to observe and note what went on. The Carnival Committee should be ashamed of encouraging such j – frivolity."

"Come on Aggie," said Nora, "they were nobbut laikin'. It did no harm. Though yan or two might have caught a cold. It was a bit chilly that day to gan oot widoot yer thermals."

More amusement, hidden behind hands and lowered eyelids.

"Thank you for your question, Aggie," said Hilary. "The dramatic performances are quite likely to be done in costume, but I think we can expect the schools to control the young people's urge to strip naked in the street."

Outright laughter.

"Oh dear," said Aggie, fanning herself, "I really must go. It must be time for my medication." And with that, she got clumsily to her feet, dragged her handbag off the chair, and blundered out.

Avis stood up then and proposed that if Hilary would give them the date of the Festival for their diaries, everyone could have tea and carry on chatting. Nora stumped off to the kitchen to encourage the hot water urn and to liberate the cakes from their cling-film.

When Hilary had outlined the various venues and the all-day-and-evening nature of the planned event, she invited a show of hands from those interested. Nora put up the hand that wasn't occupied with cling-film. Most of the ladies were willing to organise or help, including Meriel Appleby-Station, who like Nora had no ambition to sing, act, dance or recite poetry – with or without a fancy dress costume. She summed up her contribution as "blessed are the tea-makers" and as such she was satisfied.

9 :: The Coffee Morning Circuit

One of Dangleby's greatest assets was the Coffee Morning circuit. Various stalwarts womanned the Memorial Hall kitchen in order to pour hot drinks and dispense scones and cakes, in aid of the Red Cross, the Air Ambulance, the local doctor's surgery, occasional animal charities, and whichever famine or disaster relief fund was current. The Fat Cat Café, realising the impossibility of competing with volunteer labour, had reduced its morning openings to Monday and Wednesday, and specialised instead in farmhouse lunches and afternoon teas.

Nora's contribution to Coffee Mornings was to wield the aluminium teapot, a container of such mighty capacity that it required a second handle on the leading edge. Her many years of farm work had endowed her with upper body strength the equal of most men's and her alarmingly brisk action with the teapot was the stuff of legend. David Walker's brown store coat was said to have acquired its colour from "stewing in Nora's pot" and small children to have developed freckles from her "cornering" accidents.

"Can we rely on you, Nora?" the organisation's chairwoman would ask, and Nora would respond, "Aye, God willin'."

And as the chairwoman thanked her everyone would feel a sense of relief, because if Nora handled the teapot, she could be excused from offering her lardy scones, and only after Christmas was there any danger from her dense fruit cake.

Aggie Tate was also a Coffee Morning volunteer, flitting with the Hall's red-banded cups between the coffee tin, the hot water urn and the milk jug. Her path crossed Nora's with the accuracy of choreography and they managed a constant flow of chit chat as they went. However, since Aggie's thin voice did not carry, the Coffee Morning regulars could only pick up Nora's half of the conversation. When Aggie reported to Nora that Mrs Dobson's churchgoing soprano had finally cracked and she was reduced to bellowing the hymns an octave lower, Nora interpreted Aggie's critical remark about "singing Methody alto" as "the rhythm method also" which gave rise to some very strange rumours in the cloisters of Pullet St Mary.

"I believe Mr Station went to the police the other day," confided Aggie as they shared the washing up towards the end of a Mountain Rescue morning. (Nora knew that this meant *"I sat at the window till Sergeant Postlethwaite came out, then I buttonholed him till he made something up to get rid of me."*) "I heard he had trouble with boys getting into the garden, again."

"Well it won't be our Wayne. He's not the sharpest tool in the box but even he knows Ah'd clatter his lugs, an' so would our Jonty. And so would our Joss if 'e were still alive, God rest 'im."

"Poor Mr Station," said Aggie, absorbed in the memory of Richard striding past her window and down the road to the Sergeant's house. "He must love his garden very much."

Nora dumped a stack of warm, newly dried saucers back into the cupboard. "Ah don't know if he does or not, but yon mop headed young gardener seems fair catched wi' Missus Station."

Aggie's teacloth paused and she lowered her voice still further. "I wondered about that myself. Alan goes there FAR more often than Ernie Braithwaite used to do. That's what college does for you, I suppose."

"Oh, college," said Nora dismissively. "That'd be why he keeps writin' them daft letters in t' *Messenger*."

Each lady heard the rattle of the other's epistolary quill in this remark.

"Boggarts," said Aggie. "Ridiculous."

"Black puddings," said Nora with a snort. "Didsta read the thing he put in this Sat'd'y? Ah'd be ashamed to give mi-sel away wi' such rubbish." She pulled a copy of the *Messenger* from her canvas bag and leafed steadily through the pages, licking her thumb at each turn. "Aye, here t'is."

~ ~

Dear Mrs ... (Sorry, I recycled my Messenger before I had read it and I can't just recall your name.)

Thanks to contacts made through your paper I have now had several sightings of the Pullet St Mary boggart for my NVQ Level 3 WGC. I thought I would let you know that there is an entirely new species, the Pullet St Mary Black Pudding, living wild on the site of the proposed bypass. I would like to use your column to ask readers to express their support for the preservation of its habitat! Demand that work on the bypass be suspended!

Yours, Alan Eversoe-Slightly, NVQ 2 WGC.

~ ~

"Whatever those fancy letters mean, they don't stand for brains, do they?" said Aggie.

"He's tekkin' the Mickey," pronounced Nora. She shook out the rinsing water from the monster teapot and put it back in the cupboard. "Tryin' to show off how clever he is, that's what I reckon. Or mebbe puttin' us off guard before he brings out his master plan. This year Dangleby… next year, Pullet St Mary. You watch yourself, Agnes Tate. He could be going to snatch you away and fatten you up, ready to be sold as a toy to some rich oil sheik. That reminds me, Ah need some black pudden for the Hunt Supper. Ah'd best be off before George the butcher moves his van."

10 :: STRAP

A week later Alan finished his morning's work at The Grange, shouldered his rucksack, and cycled down to the Post Office.

David greeted him cheerfully. "What can I get you, young man?"

"A packet of oatcakes and a book of second class stamps please. And a *Messenger.*" He took a copy from the stack and laid it on the counter, with the oatcakes.

David fished out his key and let himself into the glass and steel cupboard where Post Office business was transacted. He had never been the victim of a hold-up. He thought that very likely if he were, the door would be locked and he would be on the outside, and the best he could hope for would be that Nora Forthright would barge into the shop and put the perpetrator in the kind of headlock she was accustomed to use on sheep. Nevertheless, he appreciated the Royal Mail's efforts to safeguard him.

He released a book of stamps from the rubber banded stack and Alan gave him a £5 note and enquired if there was any post for The Grange.

David, reckoning change, shook his head. "We're not allowed to discuss people's post, you know. Stuff comes in, we look after it, direct it to the right place, and stuff goes out. Postie delivers it to the right addresses, that's all we do. You should know that. Why," he added, with a wink, "are you waiting for something special? Has Missus ordered you something to encourage growth?"

Alan stared at him.

"You know, fertiliser," said David, innocently.

Alan took his stamps and the oatcakes, and left.

"You forgot your *Messenger*," called David, but he was gone.

Poor young fool, he thought, chuckling. He shouldn't tease him, but it was irresistible. David opened the *Messenger* and had a look down the Letters page. Had Alan been writing more rubbish about boggarts? Oh, not this time. He was on about black puddings again:

~ ~

Dear Er

I'd like to thank all your readers who have helped me with suggestions as to what to do with the Pullet St Mary black puddings. Sadly, they seem to have abandoned their usual habitat. I haven't seen them since George the butcher tried to sell me a ticket for the Hunt Supper and I told him what to do with it. I shall of course keep you informed if I rediscover them this summer.

I am now studying the wild haggis of Upper Ewedale. This is believed to be a subspecies of the Scottish haggis but it has unevenly developed left and right legs to traverse the steep slopes of the area. It can be recognised on flat ground by its circular motion.

The mating of these haggis has never been fully recorded and I would very much like to video their spawning rituals which are said to leave large muddy circles in fields. If any farmers are out there with a mobile phone during lambing, never mind the DEFRA paperwork, insurance claim forms and vets' bills, could they please call AT ONCE to tell me about any sightings?

Yours

Alan Eversoe-Slightly, NVQ 2 WGC

~ ~

Alan wrote such earnest letters, but he never gave a telephone number or an address for people to get in touch. David couldn't decide which of his obsessions was sillier, Mrs Appleby-Station or mythological local fauna.

Thinking back on it, Alan had been strange when he called in the shop. Why did he ask about Mail for The Grange? David remembered sorting an increasing number of cheap brown envelopes addressed in square capitals to DR. R. STATION, with much emphasis on the full stops and an incorrect dot over the capital I. Some of them were bulky and fastened with sticky tape. Of course, it wasn't his job to weed out anything except unaddressed junk mail, and these envelopes were correctly addressed and stamped so they must be delivered. Still, it was odd.

Aggie Tate was at it again, too.

~ ~

Dear Editor

Does the Planning Department really think that the proposed skateboard with BMX rink is necessary? Already we have seen far too much of those young people who terrorise our pavements with their wheels, with their trousers threatening to fall down at every jump. Really one wonders what those low slung crotches are supposed to imply. I watched all day but there wasn't a clue, even from the ones who weren't English.

Even with my medication, I don't think I'll be able to stand the suspense.

Yours

Aggie Tate (Miss)

~ ~

Poor Aggie – there was something not quite right there. However, the shop bell tinkled for the entrance of a customer, so David let himself out of the Post Office cubbyhole and transformed back from Sherlock Holmes into an everyday grocer.

***

At the T junction the other side of Pullet St Mary, Alan swung his bike onto the grass verge and dismounted. He took off the dreadlocks and exchanged them for a cycle helmet out of the rucksack. He put on a high visibility waistcoat, then remounted the bike and pedalled off along the main road, head down, legs pumping, in the direction of Nether Goosethwaite.

Eight miles later, he swerved into a narrow street behind the old town gas-holder, which was being demolished prior to redevelopment into luxury apartments. Nether Goosethwaite was much larger than its sister Upper Goosethwaite, where the Agricultural College stood and where there was no shop or pub and the houses commanded high prices. By contrast Nether Goosethwaite had two supermarkets, twenty seven pubs and coaching inns, two night clubs (one on three floors) and six ethnic takeaways. And it still held dingy terraces like this, waiting to be torn down.

He dodged the tipper-trucks and dumpers, and dismounted to push the bike along a dark alleyway between two of the houses, into a walled yard. At a peeling, green-painted door he leaned over to knock a complicated pattern, then he took off his helmet and parked the bike against the kitchen wall.

After an interval of thumps and crunches, the door opened.

"Alan!" squeaked a breathless voice, and a shaven headed young woman flung out her arms to him. He lifted her off her feet in a comradely hug. Once inside, they carefully replaced the two planks that held the door shut.

In the kitchen, a youth of about Alan's own age sat leaning his elbows on a wooden table. One end, against the wall, carried a bag of muesli, a carton of soya milk, some herbal teas, and a portable gas ring whose flexible hose coiled down under the table. He, too, was shaven headed.

"Jezza just got here," said the girl. "We're trying to think of a fresh approach to the lab problem."

Alan dropped his rucksack in the least cluttered corner of the room, and dug out the packet of oatcakes. He sat opposite Jezza.

"We've got all summer to plan a proper campaign."

Rebecca lit the gas ring, and filled the kettle from a pail in the sink.

"Yeah, but we need direct action."

"Think about who should be the target, then," said Alan, and broke open the pack of oatcakes. They all took one and sat munching, unable to speak for crumbs, while the kettle worked its way up to a boil.

Jezza reached into his jute carrier and brought out a sheaf of paper and a pencil. The paper bore a hand printed heading, "Dangleby Animal Freedom Three" but this title and its acronym had long been discarded because none of the Three still lived in Dangleby. When Alan went away to college they had no base in Pullet St Mary either, and had to resort to calling themselves Stop Hunting And Grouse Shooting. So far they had tackled the grouse shooting by baiting the moors with gin-soaked raisins the night before a shoot, thus rendering the birds too drunk to fly; but this had proved a strain on their ethics – was it fair to give the birds hangovers, and was it putting them at risk with foxes? An attempt to replace the lead in shotgun cartridges with shredded paper bearing the group's acronym had failed when the paper shredder packed in. Rebecca, however, had insisted that they must be careful not to waste the earth's resources, so the cartridge contents should be saved for a later campaign, and the remaining headed papers were still perfectly good for diagrams, plans and notes.

Towards the end of Alan's course at Upper Goosethwaite, they had decided to shave their heads as a declaration of protest at the fur trade.

Now they squatted in this condemned house in Nether Goosethwaite. It was a difficult name to construct a title around, so for the moment the Three called themselves Save The Research Animal Populace.

"Did we get any response from the puppy farm?" asked Alan.

"Yeah," said Jezza. "They've put a bloody big dog on a chain at the gate."

"Bastards," said Rebecca. "Exploitation on top of exploitation." The other two nodded and looked serious. She added brightly, "But any reaction is good. It means they are *aware* of our disapproval."

She poured hot water into three cups. By the time it had cooled enough to wash down the oatcake crumbs, Jezza was onto his third sheet of paper, mostly doodles. Alan took the pencil away from him.

"Did you post the protest letters to Dr Station?"

"Yeah, two a day for the past two weeks. I sent a batch to our cell in Yorkshire and she's been posting them too. Are they getting there?"

"Dunno. The postmaster clammed up when I asked him."

"Have you seen any evidence of the effect?" Rebecca asked Alan.

"Hard to tell," he admitted. "Station's on his way to the lab long before the post arrives. Maybe his missus burns them before he gets home."

"Yeah, but do they get to her?"

"Dunno. She's a jittery sort of woman anyway, looks like she's going to burst into tears half the time."

"Yeah, but not as many times as she should have." Jezza gave a short laugh.

Alan turned on him viciously. "I sent her to you when she wanted an earthing strap, didn't I? And you only did half a job. You didn't even fasten it on properly."

"Yeah? And how was I to know the remote was faulty?"

"We never got as far as needing the remote! Those meddling kids from Dangleby knocked it down and after that a one eyed man in a sandstorm could have spotted the thing."

Rebecca said uneasily, "We should have done a sit-in protest. That would have been better than tear-gas."

"It wouldn't," said Alan. "You were only worried somebody would recognise your voice if we telephoned to claim responsibility."

"Yeah, only she never needed to phone, did she," said Jezza.

"Only cos you fluffed the job in the first place!"

Rebecca put down her mug and folded her arms. "I wasn't afraid for my personal safety, no matter what you think. I didn't like the idea of tear-gas, not when his boys were going to be at home."

"Yeah right. What are you worrying about his little brats for?"

"Jezza's right," said Alan. "Is he going to show them the mutilations, the cancers and the ulcerated eyes? Of course not. He's an animal torturer and he'll bring *them* up as animal torturers unless we convince him otherwise."

"Yeah," said Jezza. "Yeah."

"Okay," said Rebecca. "All right. And that's why we were going to do it, only it didn't work, so I vote now that we conduct a verbal abuse campaign. We can stand and chant at him and at passers by."

"Oh Bex, do grow up. His house is stuck out on the edge of the village. Who'd take any notice?"

"We could do it outside the lab," she said. "If we could find out which one he's working in at the time."

"Yeah."

"I can only find that out from inside," said Alan.

Rebecca said, "You don't have to be on the inside. Did the police question you about the tear-gas? If they suspect anything we'll have to draw back, and work from a distance."

He shook his head. "They just asked a few questions. Took fingerprints. That place is like Fort Knox with all those cameras. We've got to find out Station's plans, and like I said, I can only do that from inside. The wife trusts me." He didn't mention his suspicion that Meriel would like to do more than trust him. "That's how I got to know about her wanting the earthing strap. You did use gloves, didn't you?" he asked Jezza.

Jezza said, "Yeah. Well, most of the time. It was fiddly." He looked down at his mug.

"What's the use," said Alan, in despair. "You're lucky it was only that beef-eater Postlethwaite doing the investigating."

Jezza stuck his chin out. "Yeah? So what's your next big idea then?"

"Well, as a matter of fact..." Alan sat back on his chair. The back fell off and he fell with it. Rebecca jumped to help him up, the table wobbled and the kettle fell off the gas ring.

Jezza laughed and flicked the spilt water at them.

"Oh shut up," said Rebecca. "All you ever want is to see someone get hurt. So long as it isn't you."

"Hush," said Alan, standing up and rubbing his elbow. "The next thing we do will work. And," he reassured Rebecca, "it won't hurt anybody, and it *will* help the research animals."

12 :: Wayne versus Zak

Wayne found he didn't want to play with Zak any more. He didn't quite know why. After the failed pirate raid on The Grange, the sight of Zak in the school yard or the classroom produced complicated emotions. Words like betrayal hadn't yet found their way into his consciousness. He didn't know that he was resentful about the way Zak had cut and run without even a backward glance. He didn't know that he felt guilty about enjoying Zak's humiliation – and that word certainly wasn't part of his vocabulary. But at playtime now he avoided him, and when Zak coaxed him at the end of the afternoon to go home to play video games, he just kept walking till Zak was too out of breath to follow.

The next Monday, three other new boys joined the school, and Zak dropped Wayne completely. Wayne had a couple of rough playtime exchanges with this new Pirate Crew, and took to hanging around in the safe zone near the duty teacher. At the end of the day, instead of wandering the streets of Dangleby, he went straight to his Grannie Nora's.

"You again?" she sniffed, when he tapped at her door with his shoulders hunched against a steady spring rain. "Well, come in. Did yer Dad send yer? No? What yer done this time then?"

She shut the door behind him with a thump, and he grinned a little. Gruff though she might be, she was his stronghold.

By the end of the week Nora had accepted that Wayne was visiting her willingly and not because Jonty shook a big stick at him. She adapted her daily routine to include him. "Come on, git your skates on, Ah need some flour. Git yersel down to David Walker's and fetch me three pound." And by the next Monday she'd started to say, "Git yersel some sweeties wi' t'change."

A little later, she said, "What's yer Dad having for tea then?" and included Wayne in cooking some of her trademark scones.

When he carried home that first box-full of warm, misshapen discs, the glow of successful creation battled with apprehension. Would his Dad like them? Then he worried that his Dad would know how many Wayne had eaten on the way home. Luckily, it was an evening when Jonty was busy silaging till gone ten o'clock, so Wayne was asleep and didn't see the expression on his Dad's face when he encountered Nora's heavy, lardy recipe once more.

In the morning, Jonty had washed the box out, and told him to take it back. Wayne didn't push his luck by asking for a judgement on his cooking. He did peek into the kitchen bin, but Jonty could have dumped the scones on the fire, fed the birds with them, given them to a stray dog, flushed them down the toilet, anywhere – so he had no idea whether his Dad had eaten them or not.

Weekends were trickier than school days. If his Dad worked on a Saturday, Bert Askew was grudging about Wayne dogging Jonty's footsteps through the working day. Wayne was similarly reluctant to follow Nora to her Coffee Morning duties in the Memorial Hall kitchens, where he might meet Aggie Tate or Meriel Appleby-

Station or both. Accepting that he wasn't wanted anywhere else, he went to football practice.

On the first Saturday it was raining. Attendance was down. Mr Benson set him to sprinting and dodging with the rest of the group round sets of plastic cones, then he was paired with Tom Spencer, the only coloured boy, to practise ball exercises. The rain came down and the grass became browner and slippier. Everything seemed to Wayne to be about physical strength and control, but as he had speed in plenty, he didn't find it too difficult.

When he and Tom got to play for a few minutes on a five aside team, his approach to the game was revealed, ancient in its simplicity. If he got possession he put his head down and ran for goal. Mr Benson shouted advice. Opposing players took the ball off him. As they jogged back up the field after a goal by the other side Tom tried to explain about strategy, but it simply didn't make sense to Wayne. He felt no resentment, only a kind of wondering admiration. Perhaps understanding would arrive with another birthday. He didn't make the team for Sunday.

At the end of that morning he ran home, dumped his wet kit in the washing machine, and watched children's TV. And some horse racing. He moved the washing into the clothes dryer, and watched more children's TV.

It was still raining on Sunday and Jonty had agreed to do overtime to mend one of the silage trailers. Wayne watched some of his Dad's DVDs, but he didn't understand most of them and all that television made him feel drowsy and ill tempered. He would have gone round to Grannie Nora's, but the WI had gone on a coach trip to a jam factory. All the following week Nora's practised making jam tarts and Wayne practised eating them.

The next Saturday was a fine one, so everybody who had missed football practice last week turned up on account of the sunshine. He outran most of the other boys in the fitness exercises, despite a week of jam tarts. Mr Benson tried to explain the purpose of marking opponents, and Wayne did his best to understand, but Tom's Mum collected him early to go to a dramatic rehearsal, and at that point Wayne gave up and just ran, without trying to think at the same time.

He walked home this time considering the possibilities of children's TV, and realised that he was still itching to do something. He dumped his kit, wrapped a jam tart in an immense amount of cling-film, then stuffed tart and fists into his jeans pockets, and went out again.

He scuffled and kicked stones along the Backs, the road behind the terraced houses of Dangleby. The Backs were gravelled and stone-walled, originally built just wide enough for a horse and cart to deliver to the yards. As he danced and dodged he kept a wary eye on Ernie Hodgson's house, where Alan Eversoe-Slightly lodged in the spare room. He noticed Aggie Tate's neat black cat on top of the wall in the sunshine. It considered him, and drew up from couchant to a sitting position. Wayne abandoned his dribbling-practice, and walked up to the wall, where the cat was at eye level.

He could hear boys playing on the main street, but it was quiet on the Backs. No curtains twitched, and nobody shouted. He glanced each way, then he put his elbow on the wall top, and wiggled a finger at the cat.

"How do, Puss," he said. The cat arched its back and stretched, and padded, heavy-footed but silent, to push up a wet nose and curving whiskers to investigate him. He tickled its head carefully, and the cat sat up on its haunches to rub against his hand and purr, three-thrum, three-thrum.

"You're a nice Puss, you are."

He heard a crunch of gravel and drew back his hand, thinking that he heard Aggie coming back from her coffee morning duties to shout at him. *You, boy, stop teasing my cat.* But it wasn't. It was Zak and his Pirates, on bikes.

Zak on a BMX, wearing a pack-of-sausages helmet in lime green, was a terrible sight. His expanse of denim bottom smothered the saddle and his expensively trainer-shod feet stuck out at forty five degrees. But he grinned at the sight of Wayne and the affectionate cat, and he eased clumsily to a halt and put his feet down. He said something to his new mates, and they looked at Wayne and laughed.

Wayne's heart began to pound. He knew a threat when he saw it.

Two of them dropped their bikes and ran towards him, and he balled his fists and backed against the wall but they ran round him. They glanced sideways just long enough to make a point before they slowed and sidled up to the wall from his other side. The cat rolled over in the sunshine, stretched its claws and looked at them from under one paw.

Wayne realised they had surrounded him and they were closing in. They laughed again then, hands readying themselves as they looked at each other and back to Zak for instructions – strange, excited laughter.

Zak shouted, "Catch it, you dummies."

They came in fast. Wayne had shut his eyes, so it took him a moment to realise that they had gone past him to seize the cat. It didn't struggle at first, until one took its front paws, and the other its back legs. Then it jerked and bit at their hands. Wayne stifled a protest. He had been too slow, and now that they'd caught the cat he was afraid to add to its distress.

They took no notice of him.

"Hold it still," said Zak. "C'mon, stupid, put it on the ground. And you..." – to the boy on the other bike – "you come after me. Let's see how Auntie Tate likes this."

The two boys held the cat down on the gravel. It bit hard now, and twisted and snarled. They were made clumsy by its struggles but they didn't let go, and when it was stretched out on the ground Zak and the other boy put their feet on the bike pedals and pushed off towards it.

Two things happened at once. The cat screamed and convulsed and got a paw free to claw its captors, and as though it had clawed him too Wayne slitted his eyes and charged at the leading bike. Cat and captors separated in front of him, the cat fleeing with a wild cry, the two boys clutching bloody scratches in their forearms. Zak came on, head-down, arse-in-air, pedalling for all he was worth. Wayne sprinted straight at him. He sank one fist into the dough of Zak's belly, and got a crack on the nose from the rim of Zak's helmet. They tumbled over sideways, drawing an arc of lime green along the wall. A pedal – or maybe a foot, or a stunt bar – caught Wayne's shin, and he fell right over Zak, rolling across the gravel, escaping by inches as the second bike crashed into the first. His hands grated across stone, but he rolled on and up onto his feet. A man's voice shouted in one of the yards, and before the Pirate Crew could turn and follow Wayne ran, limping, sobbing, down the Backs onto the side street, round the corner and away to Grannie Nora's.

In his flight he could think of no-one else to save him. When he got to the doorstep he panicked that the house might be locked, but the handle turned and gave. He dived in and slammed and bolted the door.

He sat for several minutes panting on the doormat, wiping his bloody nose and hugging his scraped hands and knees. He listened. Bike tyres went past, voices argued, shouted, feet skidded on tarmac. The tyres turned and came back down the lane, voices dared each other to bang on the windows and rattle the doorknob. Wayne sat behind the solidity of the door, unseen and silent. Zak and the Crew swore at each other and he could hear them arguing about whether Nora was in. After a minute or two they stopped and Wayne's heart rate went up again as he wondered what the silence might mean. But they picked up their bikes and hared off back towards the main street.

Wayne stayed quiet. As his breathing cleared he was comforted by Nora's scrubbed and polished house smell. He sucked his grazed palms, and hoped that the cat had got home all right. It was a nice cat. It had trusted him. It didn't know that Zak wanted to run over it.

Sitting there on the prickly coconut matting, he discovered that he hated Zak.

When Nora came home she had to rattle the doorknob and shout at him to let her in. He flipped the bolt, jumped up from behind the door, and clutched at her with passionate hands. Only when she held him close to her soapy, tweed-buttoned body did he give way to tears.

13 :: The Parade

The Dangleby and Pullet St Mary Literary, Music, Dance and Drama Festival blew in on a shiveringly cold wind.

"Flaming June," grumbled Hilary Tiverton-Dick, as she hauled her costume over a comfortable brown jumper and trousers. "If this is global warming, I'll eat Paul Mooney on toast."

She completed her character of Winnie the Pooh's friend Owl by slinging on her church-choir gown, together with an old pair of round spectacles, and a fleecy hat to which she had stitched a pair of upstanding ear-tufts. Her husband Phil was snuggling into corduroy trousers and a false beard, as Peter Rabbit's enemy Mr McGregor. Privately each thought the other looked terrifying.

Phil carefully packed his camera, accessories and digital voice recorder into the boot of Hilary's vintage orange Capri. He was as good a reporter as Hilary, albeit with camera rather than words, and would be her alter ego today among the spectators. He seldom missed the snippets that would make good 'hooks' for a story, and usually took telephone numbers so Hilary could glean more details. Between them they made their tiny local newspaper as good as many in bigger towns.

Hilary dumped her clipboard onto the back seat, and they set off for the Cloisters of Pullet St Mary for the first event of the day.

"Are you sure you don't want a lift when I go back to Dangleby?" she asked, as she steered carefully past the groups of costumed children.

"No, I'd rather walk with the Parade," he said. "You rush back to Dangleby for your authors."

She nodded, and swung the car into the park by the Cloisters. They got out and separated into the gathering, each bound for their own tasks. Hilary billowed away in her gown to introduce the choreographer from Manchester to the dancers, their parents and their lady instructor. Phil strolled among the spectators, asking what their costumes represented, and taking photographs. One mum held the hands of two children dressed as Teletubbies, while PC Plum trotted beside Bob the Builder. Phil got good shots of them and asked a few questions, holding out the digital recorder for names and costume details. He moved on. He was struck by the surreal appearance of three half naked Egyptians, wearing wigs made of trimmed mop heads and pushing a pram chassis on which lay a full-size, rigid bandage-wrapped mummy. When they saw Phil framing his picture, they turned shy, and behind their half-masks their turquoise-painted eyelids dipped in sideways glances at each other. He asked a few deliberately uninformed questions. Were they sand-dancers? Were they Antony and Cleopatra? Was the mummy King Tut-ankh-amun? But when they stayed dumb despite the invitation of the voice recorder, he gave up and laughed at himself. Perhaps his most pressing question, "Why the pram?" had been too obvious to answer. They pushed their strange load away, and he turned to frame them again in a long shot of the Parade which was forming on the far side of the Cloisters.

***

Nora Forthright had foregone the Parade, arguing that she had jobs to do in the house before she went out, and she wasn't going to walk to Pullet St Mary and walk back when she would be on her feet for the rest of the day with the teapot. However, Wayne begged her to wear a grey-brown woolly tea-cosy, hardly more shapeless than her usual headgear, and over her face a cone of brown cardboard with a black nose on the end (painted by himself). These, together with her tweed coat, would turn her into a redoubtable Mrs Tiggywinkle. But she wouldn't try them on for him. She gave him a collection of fifty pence pieces and chased him off out.

Wayne added her donation to the pocket money his Dad had given him for the day, and ran down towards the Fat Cat Café, where Jade and her Mum were doing face painting.

"What do you want to be?" they asked him. He had no idea. He was only their second customer so there was nobody he could point to and say, "Make me look like that."

They flicked through patterns in a book – clowns, mice, owls. None of them rang any bells with him.

"What are you good at?" asked Mrs Braithwaite helpfully, the brush cocked between her fingers. Wayne found it difficult to think of anything in particular. "Cooking scones and jam tarts" didn't strike him as a useful answer. Then he thought of football, and eventually he found a word.

"Running," he said.

"Well, there you are then. With that hair, you'll be perfect as a cheetah."

It was hard for him to keep still and the makeup felt odd but the effect, when he looked in the mirror, was startling. He made a snarly face, and Mrs Braithwaite laughed.

Afterwards, he swaggered out among the stalls that lined the street. Balloons and windmills rattled in the breeze, masks and gaudy toys sat next to second-hand books, art prints and home made cakes. He by-passed the card making and other children's activities, feeling that his masked face and painted whiskers were put to better use in sprinting along the street, and dancing and stalking and spitting at people. Then he saw Zak.

Zak was costumed in red and purple with a turban on his head, and Mrs Tate appeared to be propelling him towards Pullet St Mary to meet the Parade. Wayne had never seen *Aladdin*, so he only thought Zak looked like a raspberry jelly, but as soon as Zak began to shout he dived into cover behind a second-hand book stall.

He found Tom Spencer there, out of the stallholder's line of sight, reading.

"Hullo," said Tom, shutting the Top Gear book. "Wow, that's a really cool face."

Tom had shiny brown skin and curly hair. The two boys, dark and fair, studied each other with friendly curiosity. Wayne knew that Tom's Mum was even more brown. She came from somewhere called Zimbabwe, but his Dad was from Pullet St Mary, so Tom's slightly singsong way of delivering a sentence was mixed with his Dad's familiar Cumberland vowels. He could be forgiven for attending a different school, because he was sometimes picked for the Sunday football team.

"Thanks," said Wayne. He noticed that Tom was wearing a Manchester United shirt under his jacket. "Why aren't you dressing-up?"

"I am dressed-up."

"You're not!"

"It's good enough to do a reading. I don't need to dress up for that."

"What's a reading?" Wayne had managed to avoid getting involved with any of his class's literary work and his contribution to the dramatic side had been to smear paint on a few masks. He had no qualms about not joining the Parade as part of Dangleby school. It was less exacting to remain a free lance and besides, it kept him away from Zak.

"Mrs Hunter let us choose a book we liked and we read some of it out in class. I think she likes my voice," said Tom, "cos she picked me to read in the Hall this afternoon, me and Ellen and Joshua. We're all doing bits from *The Golden Compass*. I'm going to read about the polar bear – you know – Iorek Byrnison – and how Lyra got his armour back."

Wayne, who had never read anything by Philip Pullman, just said, "What you doin' till then?"

The stallholder cleared his throat irritably, and Tom put the book down. He said, "There's a Robin Hood stall over the other side of the cricket pitch. They let you use real bows-and-arrows. I've got some money. C'mon!"

***

Meriel had been allocated the early shift in the Memorial Hall alongside Aggie Tate. Some of the other ladies had promised to join them once their children had performed their dances and songs, but there wasn't much custom yet, just a few people popping in to complain of the cold wind and sit down for a cup of tea. Meriel expected there would be a rush when the Parade came over from Pullet St Mary, then it would quieten before lunch time when Nora and Avis would come to take over. That meant she would be free in the afternoon to watch while Richard read the part of Mr Dicey in the Dangleby Scribblers' parody, *Price and Prejudice.* While she had never read Jane Austen's novel and had no interest in filling the gap in her knowledge, Richard was enthusiastic so she felt she ought to make an effort. She wouldn't need to pay too much attention, just be visible in the audience. And perhaps she would see Alan among the spectators.

She hoped Robbie and Jamie didn't mind too much that Richard had not brought them home for the weekend. At first he had only said rather crossly that he couldn't drive to fetch the boys from St Gullible's, as well as read in the Scribblers play, and practise in the cricket nets that evening.

She had protested, "But I could fetch the boys, Richard. They'd so love to dress up and buy rubbish from the charity stalls!"

Richard had looked at her with a tinge of impatience. "I know, but you're not going to."

She sat down at the kitchen table, disappointed. She debated giving way to tears; sometimes Richard was easy to move if she cried. However, she suspected that this time his mind was made up, so she just said, "Oh."

"Look, Merry, there will be people here in their hundreds – people we don't know and can't trust. How many of our friends could we recognise, if they were in costume? I don't feel comfortable about the boys wandering the streets."

"Oh, Richard, I do think you're exaggerating. That sort of thing only happens in cities. Who would want to hurt our darling boys?"

"Remember the package they found under the Disco," he said, and his dark eyes were steady and serious.

"Do you really think –?" began Meriel. "Was that what all those letters were about? Darling, do be reasonable."

"Merry," he said with some exasperation, "why do you think I have security cameras all round the place? Why did the police take me seriously when I worried about those boys climbing in all the time? You still haven't worked out what they found, have you? For God's sake, Merry, it was a grenade. A tear-gas grenade. We were just lucky it fell off before they could activate it. These animal activists are extreme. They're *not* reasonable. They'll hurt us if they can, even if it's only by accident."

"But you changed your job, darling! Just for me! You were so sweet about it."

"I don't think they realise that. And to be honest I don't think they'd care – even if I stuck up a placard with the facts on it, they'd say it was just a bluff. People like that keep on. So we either keep the boys away until the activists are caught, or we make up our minds to move again."

She had clasped her hands to her throat, and nodded.

He said, "You just stick close to Ma Forthright and that silly old Tate woman when you're doing your good deeds with the fairy cakes."

She whispered, with an attempt at a smile, "I shall ask dear Alan if he will look after me."

Richard had pulled her to her feet and kissed her savagely. "Don't you bloody dare," he said, and gave her bottom a warning spank.

***

Aggie broke in on her musings. "It's half past ten, Mrs Station."

"Appleby-Station," said Meriel automatically, but the vague smile returned, the polite mask in place. "Do you think we should brew a fresh pot?"

"Well, it's not for me to say, but the Parade was starting off from the Cloisters at ten and it's nearly half past now."

"Jolly good," said Meriel, clopping across to the sink. The water heater was hissing comfortably so she tipped out the stewed tea from the teapot, squeezed the used teabags and threw them in the bin, and rinsed the pot with hot water. "Tally ho," she said cheerily, and popped fresh bags into the pot.

Aggie stiffened. 'I believe that is a hunting expression."

"Oh, I'm so sorry," said Meriel. "I beg your pardon, I quite forgot. How is your sweet old pussy?"

Aggie had turned away and was putting out cups and saucers on the counter.

"Catkin recovered quite well from her ordeal with the hounds, thank you. Though the other week she had a narrow escape of quite another kind."

"Did she?" said Meriel, through the hiss of steam as she filled the pot. "That's nice."

"Ernie Hodgson told me. I really must have a word with my brother's daughter in law."

Meriel was hopelessly confused by the tangle of relationships in Dangleby, so she didn't try to work out who this was. She put the lid on, and encouraged Aggie with a lift of her eyebrows.

"Young Isaac tried to run over my poor Catkin on his bicycle, along the Backs. And him my own great-nephew!"

Meriel completed her task and trotted back to the counter, where Aggie swathed the pot in a tea towel. "Oh, surely not."

"Oh, most certainly Yes!" said Aggie. "Isaac certainly got some of what he deserved – one of the boys assaulted him. I shall write a strong letter to the *Messenger* about the falling standards of behaviour among our children. Then I must make the episode known to his mother. I daresay she is only in possession of half the facts."

Meriel opened the cupboard and brought out a tray of sugar-bowls, each crammed with packets of sweeteners, sauces, salt and pepper. She smiled over it, and said vaguely, "Of course. Do you think we should put the condoms on the tables now?"

14 :: The Play

Sergeant Postlethwaite, David Walker and a couple of Post Office customers watched from the shop doorway as the Parade straggled its way into Dangleby. Led by the Pullet St Mary Silver Band playing the overture to "The Gondoliers," it passed Nora's house and the Post Office and trailed round the corner onto the main street.

David was mildly amused by the costumes, some of which had started life in his shop as plain papier-mâché masks and were now inventively painted. The Year 1 school children dressed as characters from Beatrix Potter's books made him chuckle, and when Nora Forthright joined them in her brown tea-cosy and Mrs Tiggywinkle snout he had to go and hide behind the door in order to laugh.

Sergeant Postlethwaite nodded to his two constables, strolling along beside the Parade. In a moment David came out again, with his face readjusted into polite approval.

"I hope my lads are keeping an eye on the fat boy," said the Sergeant, in an undertone to David.

"Him with the turban? Looks like his mother's laying down the law to him."

"High time. I've had a few words with him myself recently."

When Aggie Tate heard of the attack on her cat she had flown round to the police station with her usual promptness. The Sergeant, satisfied for once that she had grounds for complaint, had interviewed Zak and the other Pirates and their families, and issued them with cautions.

"I don't know how she copes with him," said David. He could see that Zak was in a foul temper.

Sergeant Postlethwaite folded his arms in disapproval. "It's a great pity she and Tony are both out at work at the end of his school day."

Zak pulled off his purple turban and stamped on it. PC Plum, behind them, picked it up and ran to hand it back. Mrs Tate tried to push it onto Zak's head, but when Zak knocked her hands away it began to unwind. The Egyptians danced by with their mummy on the pram chassis, saying nothing, and the Parade moved onward and round the corner out of sight.

***

Meriel was soon busy in the Memorial Hall, and as the morning wore on she was cautiously pleased by Mrs Tate's early arrival with an offer to clear dirty cups and plates, and to wipe down tables. Meriel was nervous of Mrs Tate, aware that she was the mother of the fat trespasser whom Richard had walloped with the cricket bat, but she remembered her husband's outburst this morning and tried hard not to say anything.

For Aggie, however, Mrs Tate was close family, and she did not scruple to accuse Zak, in bursts between her journeys with trays from the counter to the sink.

"Far be it from me to criticise – I really don't think you discipline that child properly – it makes me glad I have no children of my own..."

But Mrs Tate dumped another tray of crockery, exchanged her cloth for a clean one, and was off again into the cheerful hubbub of crowded tables.

Aggie bore away the debris, muttering, "I'm ashamed to have family who behave like that. Where is that child now, I'd like to know?"

Meriel suggested, timidly, that perhaps Zak was with the school children, who were scheduled to perform in the Square, repeating the dance they had done in Pullet St Mary before the Parade.

'When did that child ever dance," sniffed Aggie. When Mrs Tate returned, she started again. "Those new boys from the far end of town – they held down my poor Catkin..."

"Well, I can't say I know them," said Mrs Tate, stolidly refusing to be drawn on the subject.

" – and Ernie said he saw Isaac on his bicycle..."

Meriel gave a little scream, and they both jumped. She was pointing to the window over the sink.

'What is it?" asked Mrs Tate, glad to be distracted from Aggie's tirade. She came into the kitchen and peered out of the window, without apparently seeing anything out of the ordinary.

"Oh, so silly of me I know. I saw a face – like a mask."

"Well, of course," said Mrs Tate, rinsing her dishcloth and wringing it out. "There are plenty about today, after all."

"Oh yes, I know. I simply didn't expect to see any round this side of the building."

"It's probably a child," said Mrs Tate. She added fondly, "I've dressed Isaac as the Sultan from the Thousand and One Nights."

"No, it was something with big dark eyes," said Meriel. "Not a child. Sort of Siamese."

Aggie, reminded of her feline theme, remarked acidly, "It had better keep out of the way of young Isaac then."

Mrs Tate said, "Tony is perfectly capable of keeping Isaac out of trouble." She wrung out the dishcloth with final, ferocious thoroughness and set off to clean another table.

***

The "Robin Hoods" turned out to be the Upper Goosethwaite Archery Club. Tom looked longingly at their big compound bows, but the men who took his money shook their heads.

"Not for beginners," they said with a laugh. "Just to look at!"

"Learn the rules first," said the bowman who took them to the shooting area. "And then we'll start. You never aim an arrow at anyone, you never shoot at animals, and you never shoot an arrow into the air."

'Why not?" asked Wayne.

"Cos you don't know who it'll hit when it comes back down," said Tom, avoiding the word "dummy" that Zak would automatically have added.

"Dead right," said the bowman. "Now let's see if you've got muscles, or just knots in cotton." The twenty pound draw of the child-sized bow made their arms wobble. "Go on – draw the string back as far as your nose and keep your left arm steady. That's the ticket."

"When do we get an arrow?" said Wayne, shutting one eye as he aimed at the target.

"When you can tell me which way round it goes."

"Duh! – with the point to the front?"

"No." The bowman grinned at them, and waited without explaining while they puzzled it out.

It was Tom who spotted that the cock-feather was a different colour. "Look, if you turn it this way, the notch of the arrow fits onto the string, see?"

They made their fingers sore drawing back the arrows to meet their noses. They paid the penalty of stung wrists when they forgot to keep their left elbows out of the way. By the time their money ran out, their arms ached from the power of the bow, but they were convinced that all they needed was practice, and as they walked back round the cricket pitch they were already trying to find ways to make their own bows. They had managed one arrow each on the target.

"I thought you might have had a bow," said Wayne, "coming from Africa and all."

"Oh, I am so sah-ree to dis-app-point you, Mis-tah Wayne." Tom rolled his eyes heavenwards. "I is not a savage."

Wayne wriggled, not quite understanding his self-mockery.

"Can you see me getting on the plane with a bow and arrows?" said Tom. "They X-ray your luggage in case you're a terrorist, so they'd have chucked me off right away."

Wayne had never flown, but he wasn't going to admit it. "Did they find any terrorists?"

"No."

"Boring."

"Not if you want to get home in one piece, it isn't."

"Whatever. Is it nice in Africa? I bet it isn't rainy all the time like it is here."

Tom spread his brown hands and grinned, inviting Wayne to take in the sunny countryside as though no other argument could be needed.

"Well yeah, it's okay, but it isn't warm, is it? Not like Africa. I wish we had animals here, wild animals like elephants and lions and things. Wasn't your Mum sad to leave?"

"No," said Tom. "We've seen too many people taken away."

"What d'you mean, taken away? Taken away where?"

Tom raised his shoulders. "Just away out of their houses."

"I bet it didn't really happen. I mean, people say we've got panthers here, eating sheep and stuff, you know, wild, and I'd like to see a panther, but nobody's ever caught one. I reckon they made that up to scare you."

"It's not made up!"

"I bet you don't know anybody who was tooken."

"They took Mr Maramba," said Tom. His voice wavered. "He was a friend. He was big and noisy and he had a huge laugh, but they took him and he didn't come back."

"Wow!" Wayne was pop-eyed with astonishment. "Couldn't you call the police?"

"I couldn't. It was a policeman that took him."

"Oh," said Wayne. "Why did they arrest him? Was he bad?"

"No. I don't know why. It wasn't a proper arrest like you have here, all controlled and polite. It was horrible. I had nightmares, and that's when Dad decided to come back to England."

"Wow," said Wayne again.

"I think he'd wanted to come back for a long time," said Tom, his voice recovering as he got away from the uneasy centre of the topic. "He said it was the last straw, and he'd find another job even if it didn't pay as well."

Tom's mobile phone rang, and they were both relieved because it broke the sombre mood. He looked at the number and sighed. "It's Mum. I'll have to answer."

Wayne raised his hands in an "okay by me" gesture and walked slowly on along the edge of the field.

"It's all right," said Tom, when he caught him up. "She's just reminding me that Mrs Hunter wants us at the Memorial Hall. We have to get ready for the reading."

"Oh," said Wayne. He wasn't interested in readings.

"But we could meet up again after. Have you got a penknife? If we could find some proper sticks we could make bows."

"I haven't got a penknife," said Wayne, but he thought of Grannie Nora, who had tools for everything. "Reckon I might know where to borrow one."

"That's cool."

"What kind of wood do we want? I wish we'd asked."

"I bet there are books in the library that would tell us."

Wayne pulled a face. "Look it up on the internet."

"I'll ask my Dad. C'mon, I've got to go." Tom set off at a run, and Wayne sprinted after him.

***

At the Memorial Hall, Tom told Wayne that he'd be busy for about an hour, and slipped into the Meeting room. Wayne was unwilling to face all the adults in the tea room across the corridor, so he prowled round the outside of the Hall until he found the kitchen door. It wasn't locked. He poked his cat-face in to look for Grannie Nora, and Meriel, who had barely recovered from the first mask at the window, clutched at her throat and squeaked, "There's another one!"

Wayne was equally startled at meeting the drug baron's wife face to face, and he nearly ran away, but Mrs Tate called him in.

"It's all right," she told Meriel. "He's Nora's grandson. Is that who you're looking for, Wayne?"

Wayne nodded, warily. Mrs Tate was standing by one of the work-tops, transferring sausage rolls, filled buns and cakes from several small plastic boxes into a very large one, which he recognised as Zak's lunch box. She seemed a bit het-up, he thought, as he watched her hands prodding the buns into place. He couldn't tell whether the agitation was normal for the Memorial Hall kitchen, or whether Zak was around, or how much Zak had told his mother of their last encounter.

"Your Grannie's just gone to wash her hands," said Mrs Tate. "I'll tell her you're here but you might have to wait."

She stopped to serve two cups of tea at the counter, then, "Don't touch anything," she said, and went out.

Meriel stayed in the kitchen, refilling the hot water jug. Now she had got over her fright at Wayne's face paint it amused her, though by breaking up the shapes of his features it made her uncertain whether she knew him or not. She smiled at him. He must be about the same age as Robbie and Jamie. Moved by a wish that they had been allowed to join in the day's fun, she offered him a can of pop from the stack on the shelf. Wayne, who was more used to irritation such as Nora and Mrs Tate displayed, distrusted such a spontaneous gesture from a stranger, and shook his head. The can might be doped. Then Meriel was called by a customer, so she left the can on the drainer and turned away to serve tea. Wayne was left by the sink, studying the can.

Despite his suspicions, it seemed quite normal. He recognised its name and logo, and its ring pull didn't appear to have been tampered with, so he opened it and drank. When his thirst was slaked, he realised that after his long morning of activity he had two other pressing needs: something to eat, and somewhere to pee. He knew he could scrounge food from Grannie Nora, if she would only hurry up, but he didn't know where the toilets were in the Memorial Hall and he didn't want to walk in among all the people to find them. Perhaps he could pee down the outside drain from the kitchen. Then as he stood there, next to Zak's lunchbox, a wicked thought came to him. Ordinarily, he would not have dared to disobey Mrs Tate's Don't Touch command, but he was learning to live up to his painted cheetah mask. He picked up the box, stepped outside and pulled the door to behind him.

A quick glance round the yard showed him that there was no-one watching. He peeled up the enormous lid of the box, picked out two fat sausage rolls and a ham bun, and set them on the windowsill. It occurred to him that Tom had kindly spent all his pocket money on their archery practice, so he picked out a couple of ham buns for him.

Then, carefully supporting the box with both hands, he peed in it.

It grew satisfyingly hot and heavy. The buns and cakes soaked everything up, and by the time he'd gone dry, tucked himself in tidily and put the lid back on he was thinking gleefully of Zak opening up a liquid lunch. He slid back into the kitchen and pushed the box onto the draining board just as his Grannie Nora stumped in through the opposite door.

"Now then you," she said. She had shed her coat, and her skirt and cardigan were now covered by a tea-spotted nylon overall. "Zak's mother said ye were here. What's up?"

"Um," he said.

"Yer up to mischief I doubt, wi' that face. What y' after?"

"Grannie, I met a – a friend, and we want to...'

"Which friend?"

"Tom Spencer from Pullet St Mary. We play football on Sat'dys." He was keeping a weather-eye on the door in case Mrs Tate came back from "washing her hands." It wasn't likely she'd be as slow as Grannie Nora about such things.

Meriel interrupted, asking Nora for tea, and Nora seized the pot and responded briskly. Wayne waited, hopping from foot to foot with anxiety, until she'd finished serving and clumped the pot down on the counter. She took up the conversation where it left off, allowing Wayne only a moment to nod or shake his head at her questions.

"Now then. This Tom Spencer. Is his Dad called Dan? Him that's come back with a black wife? Ah. And," with a piercing look from behind the sellotaped glasses, "is he a good boy?"

"He's all right is Tom, yeah."

Nora sniffed. "Ye thought Zak was all right, once-over. Aye well, better a black skin than a black heart I suppose."

Wayne ignored this. He must get his request in before Mrs Tate reappeared. "Grannie, we been shootin' arrows and we want to make bows."

"Bows and arrows? Is that what they use, in Zimbabwe?"

"No," said Wayne impatiently. "Don't be silly, Grannie. We been to see them Robin Hoods, t'other side of the cricket pitch. They've tellt us we've got to be careful, we know what we're doin' – honest."

Nora collected a batch of used cups and saucers from the returning Mrs Tate, and stared hard at him. She dumped the cups on the drainer, pushed the lunch box aside (Wayne's heart nearly stopped) and said, "So – what d'yer want me to do about it?"

"I haven't got a penknife," he said.

She considered this simple statement for a moment.

"Here." She dug into the pocket of her cardigan and offered him a Swiss Army knife. "I fetched it in case we had packets t' oppen. Now mind, yon's sharp. Watch yerself wi' it. Don't let Perce Postlethwaite see it either. And mind ye fetch it back in good order."

Wayne thanked her and put it carefully into his jeans pocket, wondering at his good luck.

"And I bet ye spent all yer money, didn't ye? Ye'll need t'buy some string." She gave him a pound coin. Then another customer came asking for teas, so she dusted Wayne's head and told him to be off.

He slid back out, picked the food off the windowsill and pushed it into his hoodie pockets. In the next quiet corner out of the wind he sat down and ate some of the booty. What a lot of surprising things had happened to him that morning: a new friend, a new sport, stolen food, a penknife, and most joyous of all, revenge. It was becoming a very good day.

***

Aggie had been released from her duties by the early arrival of Nora, and she stood in the chilly sunshine debating whether to have her lunch at home, or in the Memorial Hall, or at the Fat Cat Café. The Hall was still busy, but most of the customers were people she didn't know well enough to share a table with. The face painters had left the Fat Cat to enjoy the fun on the street, and service of meals had resumed. She decided to go to the Fat Cat and treat herself to a proper knife-and-fork lunch. With luck and a sharpened elbow she would get a window seat, where she could view the Square in comfort as the Scribblers prepared for *Price and Prejudice.* They were talking together, leafing through scripts, putting on scraps of costumes, a hat here, a pair of gloves or a scarf there. She thought that tall, dark Richard Station was a wonderful choice for the part of Mr Dicey.

***

The three Egyptians were huddled with their pram in the alley between the Memorial Hall and the buildings of the Square. The mummy, despite its lively travels during the morning, was still firmly fixed in place. It appeared to be made of plaster of Paris bandages.

"I'm cold," said the smallest Egyptian, arms wrapped round its half-naked torso. "This isn't what I call a costume for an English summer."

"It's perfect for what we're doing," said the tallest. "Focus."

"Yeah," said the third.

***

When Meriel was relieved by Avis, she sat in the Memorial Hall kitchen and had a cup of tea and a sandwich, and chatted for ten minutes while her feet calmed down. Then she put on her country jacket and clopped out into the cold wind of the Square.

"Glad I's not a brass monkey," said one of the spectators, as she joined the back of the crowd.

"Yes, it is cold, isn't it, very," she said. "Are they nearly ready, do you think?"

"Aye, pretty soon be t'look on it," said the woman, studying her Programme of Events. "Not that it's much of a thing, to read a play off a piece of paper."

"They have been reversing quite hard," said Meriel nervously, but the woman took no notice.

"They'll not start yet, mind, not till t'kiddies have finished reading inside."

The crowd collected round the Scribblers' arena, marked out with traffic cones and plastic tape. Meriel found she couldn't easily see anything except her husband's dark head. She stepped back a little, and noticed a handy flower tub at the base of a lamp standard. She prepared to climb up to assess whether that afforded a better view.

"Now!" said a voice behind her.

Before she could look round, hands clamped down on her mouth and the nape of her neck. She tried to scream, but other hands seized her elbows and lifted her, and more hands gripped her ankles. As she drew breath to try to scream again the hand on her mouth was replaced with a large sticky plaster and someone pulled a woolly hat over her head. It didn't quite cover her eyes, but her captors tilted her over and carried her away, face down, so that all she saw were their sandalled feet staggering across the cobbles. They spun her again and lifted her and put her down.

"Tie her knees, quickly," said the voice, "and her hands. No, *behind* her back."

Meriel protested inside her gag. The woolly hat was pulled lower and completely shut off the view, and someone wrapped her wrists in cloth. There was a grating noise, like concrete being scraped with a knife, and they lifted her a third time and laid her flat inside something whose smell reminded her of the skiing holiday when she had broken her wrist. Almost at once the grating noise was repeated and the sunlight that had flickered through the woolly hat vanished into total blackness. The container – whatever it was – rumbled and bumped along over the cobbles. She began to panic. It was very uncomfortable lying with her hands beneath her back, and from the way her elbows touched the sides as it jolted along, her prison was narrow, like a coffin.

A girl's voice said, "Start dancing, guys, somebody's coming."

Meriel tried her best to scream, but three voices chanting drowned her out, and the coffin kept on rolling. When the rapid jolting of the cobbles gave way to the wider-spaced joints of pavement, she screamed again, but through the gag it came out as no more than a high pitched growl.

The first voice said close to her ear, "Shut up, Mrs Station, and you won't get hurt."

She knew that voice now. She almost sobbed with relief. It was dear Alan, the gardener.

15 :: Laying the Trail

Aggie Tate sat in the Fat Cat Café and told herself that she was wrestling with her conscience.

She was actually watching *Price and Prejudice*, where Mr Dicey, the poor but honest chemist of Meryton, was suffering torments over competition from a local supermarket. From her slightly elevated position in the café she had a much better, warmer and altogether more private view of Richard Station than most of the audience. She had no interest in the Scribblers' dialogue or why Richard wrung his hands or struck his brow as he read. She nibbled at pie, peas and mash, and gazed at him, absorbing enough pleasure for a week.

She had seen Meriel take her place at the back of the crowd near the three young men who had been wandering round Dangleby all morning, scantily dressed as extras from Aida. Those had provided more good reasons for Aggie to remain behind the discreet glass of the Fat Cat's window. Now she noticed that Meriel had gone.

Aggie pleated the unused pink paper napkin into fine folds as she tried to decide what to do. She was hungry to continue adoring Richard Station; but surely she ought to tell him what she knew? Or should she keep it secret? Despite her two years of study, she had never actually spoken to him outside the protective rampart of the cricket club tea trestles, and she had no idea of his character outside the team. She knew his reputation as an active batsman and fielder but when she tried to picture his response to her message she found it an impossible exercise. Would he believe her? Would he be grateful? Would he be furious with her? Would he be furious with Meriel? She didn't know, but it was safer not to risk him being furious at all.

She decided it might be easier to compose an anonymous letter, on the lines of her frequent correspondence with the Messenger:

To Whom it May Concern – (too impersonal)

Or

Dear Mr Station? (possibly)

Or

Dear Richard? (Here, Aggie shivered with anxiety at her own presumption, and finally substituted *My Very Dear Sir*)

I felt I really must write to let you know that your wife

Or

– Mrs Appleby-Station –

Or

the Hon. Meriel Appleby-Station – (Aggie mentally shook herself and decided this, too, could be settled later)

has been seen consorting in public with half-naked actors – (Aggie hesitated, as she wasn't sure of their identity)

Or

thespians –

Or

drama students – (this seemed the best choice)

at the Dangleby and Pullet St Mary Literary etc etc...

She was sure that the Honourable Meriel must have gone off with them. Meriel had been watching the play from the edge of the Square, and so had they. However, Aggie's gaze had been drawn to Richard Station's performance and it wasn't until he gave his cue to the next speaker that she had glanced away and seen that Meriel had gone, and so had they. She sat at the window and continued to watch, pleating the paper napkin, while she enjoyed sympathising in spirit with poor Richard, whose wife was deceiving him so blatantly. And when the performance came to an end, she made her mind up: a letter would take too long. She would call at the police station and pass her message on that way. She knew Sergeant Postlethwaite very well by now.

***

Meriel's thoughts, if they could be called such, ran round and round in the darkness of her transport like a trapped rabbit. She was absolutely sure the voice she had heard was Alan's, but what was he doing? Why was she tied up in this – this – coffin, being rattled away to some unknown destination? Who were the other two – and one of them a girl – who appeared to be helping him to abduct her?

With the word 'abduct', a wonderfully amusing idea came to her. She remembered all the times she and Alan had been together at home, in the garden, in the shed, in the garage or – especially – in the kitchen. How shy he had seemed, how ready to blush whenever she spoke to him. With a quiver of apprehension she realised that his passion for her, so well hidden for so long, must have finally driven him to enlist his friends in carrying her off. And the Festival, where disguise was so readily accepted, had given him the perfect opportunity to do it without being recognized.

The idea was outrageous. It was delicious. She giggled, and as the narrow container continued to rumble and jolt and creak and bounce over increasingly rough going she tried to imagine how she should behave when it reached its destination – the little love nest that he had probably been preparing all these weeks.

***

Wayne had intended to greet Tom enthusiastically as he made his way out of the Meeting room of the Memorial Hall. He hadn't expected that he would have to be approved first by Tom's excitable mum. She was plump, dark skinned and dark eyed, and talking with so much vigour to Mrs Hunter that she didn't even see him.

After a minute or so, he prodded Tom and muttered, "I got a penknife." For that, he received a secret thumbs-up, although Tom's gaze remained innocently turned towards Mrs Hunter and his Mum's enthusiasm about his reading.

It was a heady feeling for Wayne. For the first time since he and his Dad had moved to Dangleby, he had secrets to tell about what he'd done, and plans for things he was going to do. He was no longer dragging his feet over what Zak wanted to do and he didn't.

He fidgeted about, trying to keep the bulging pocket of sausage rolls and buns out of sight behind Tom, until at last Mrs Spencer talked herself to a standstill and Mrs Hunter moved away to talk to another parent from Pullet St Mary.

"Well, now, Tom," said Mrs Spencer, "are you going to introduce me to your friend?"

"This is Wayne. We met at football practice."

Wayne squirmed when she offered to shake his hand. He'd never met a grown up who had done that to him. But Tom nudged him and nodded, so he put his painted paw in hers. Her palms and finger tips were pinker than the rest of her and her handshake gentler than he expected.

"How do you do, Wayne! What's your second name? Forthright? Ah! Mrs Forthright's grandson? And were you named after that boy that plays for Manchester United?"

Wayne didn't know which question to answer first, and her laughter at this was huge, like a man's. But she accepted him at Tom's word, and allowed them to go.

They dashed away, yelling and jumping across the Square, down the street, round another corner and down the Backs. As they passed Grannie Nora's house, Wayne turned a cartwheel and only remembered the buns and sausage rolls when he was upside down. He landed and shoved them back into his pocket. Broken or not, they were important because he was going to share them. He had a friend.

***

Aggie Tate marched straight up to the police station door, and bounced off. It was locked.

She avoided falling by hanging from the door handle, then righted herself and looked indignantly up and down the street. What with all the stalls of tatty old books, and balloons and – well, she had to say it, trash – it was difficult to see whether Sergeant Postlethwaite or either of his juniors was among the browsing crowd. She straightened up to a scrawny five feet one and set off towards Pullet St Mary.

***

Meriel was still being propelled along in her container. It fitted her with such closeness, she wished it had been lined with memory foam.

The lid must have slipped sideways, because prickles of light showed through the woolly hat, and she could clearly hear the grunts and gasps of her abductors. She began to wonder who the other two were, and why they were helping Alan to carry her off. He had said she wouldn't be hurt – but her elbows hurt. Her wrists hurt. Her back hurt. And she had read of strange things being done when women were kidnapped, and no doubt they had been told they wouldn't be hurt either. The girl sounded sharp and determined, and Meriel found herself listening for the other man, the one who always said, "Yeah."

Abruptly, she was thrown sideways. The lid came off, she fell with it, and three voices said, "Oh bugger."

***

Wayne and Tom finally ran out of running somewhere along the footpath which wandered through the fields from Dangleby to Pullet St Mary. They collapsed into a strip of uncut grass at the edge of Bert Askew's meadow, where scaled-out hay had dried to pale green in the afternoon sun. As they lay panting, staring up at the clouds, they could hear traffic going by on the road a couple of fields away, and beyond that, a tractor working. Wayne could tell from the noise that it was mowing. Nearer at hand a mob of small birds pursued a cuckoo down the hedge with angry cries. The smells of hay and newly mown grass drifted together on the wind.

Wayne recovered first, and sat up to investigate how badly the stolen food had fared in his pocket.

Tom looked in astonishment at the flattened sausages and crumbs, and then gave way to his family's loud laughter. "Where'd you get THEM from?"

Wayne dug deeper for the ham buns, and explained about stealing them from Zak's lunch box.

"If you hate the guy that much," said Tom, "we'd better eat as much of the evidence as we can."

They ate everything, except the flaky remains of the sausage rolls.

"I can't," said Tom 'They're just too dry."

"They're the only ones that are," said Wayne, throwing the flakes up in the air in delight at his own daring. "I peed on the rest of 'em." His accompanying mime boasted of fire-hose capacity, but the breeze blew the flakes back into his face and he had to cough them away before he could tell the full story.

"Eurgh!" Tom fell backwards into the grass. "That's wicked. Wish I'd thought of it."

After a minute Wayne said, "I wish Mrs Station had given me another can of pop."

"Yeah, I'm thirsty too." Tom sat up again and looked round. At the end of the field, the gate in the hedge stood open. "There might be water for the animals, I suppose."

They stood up and scuffled across the field through the drying hay, but the trough by the gate was almost empty, and the dregs were rust-red. Wayne considered the barn at the end of the next field. "Could be a tap up there."

He ran off up the field, followed by Tom. A double ribbon of tractor ruts led up from the gate to the concreted yard in front of the barn, and there was a trough in one corner, with a tap beside it. He turned that on, jumped back from the first brown splutter, and then leaned down to drink.

"Cor, that's better. You want some? Tom?" But Tom, for some reason, was moving stealthily to the shady side of the barn. He was watching something down the field. From weeks of piracy with Zak, Wayne recognised caution, and looked where Tom was looking.

Along the back of the hedge, they saw two Egyptians accompanying a woman in a country jacket. Wayne recognised Mrs Station and despite her kindness earlier in the day he was instantly wary, so when Tom gestured 'down' and dropped to his knees, Wayne copied him at once. Then the brown face and the cheetah mask peered round the corner close to ground level.

The Egyptians and Mrs Station moved erratically across the drying hay, heading for the gateway below the barn. She had a black woolly hat pulled down over her eyes, and after a moment, the boys realised that the Egyptians were holding on to her arms and that her hands were tied behind her back.

"Uh," said Tom. "That's not good."

Following them there was a third Egyptian with a bald head. Even at that distance, Wayne could see the rage running through his body as he struggled to steady the mummy case on top of a pram that swayed and wobbled over the grassland like a drunken man.

They ducked back into hiding and Tom whispered, "I saw them this morning. They were funny then. It was a joke. What are they coming up here for?"

"You think they are? That's Mrs Station that's with them. Her that gave me that drink in the Memorial Hall. She had that skirt on and them funny leather shoes – see? It's her all right." That was easier than having to explain his knowledge via the beech hedge and the garden of The Grange.

Tom peered round the corner again. "Whoever she is, they're coming up the track. I don't like it. ' His voice faded for a moment. "People don't tie other people up and march them across fields for a joke. C'mon. We'd better go now, before they get here."

Wayne realised that Tom was genuinely frightened. He was seeing something more, beyond Mrs Station being walked along by a trio of funny Egyptians. But Wayne's piracy with Zak had taught him a lesson or two and he stayed where he was, assessing the situation. He decided there was no cover, other than the barn itself.

"If we run now, they'll see us for certain. We'll have to stop here. That one at the back, he's as mad as fire. I don't want him catchin' me."

"No. You can bet I don't either."

"Sh."

They sat down carefully, the dark and the painted heads pressed back against the lichened wall, and listened to their hearts thumping.

***

At the end of the Scribblers' performance of *Price and Prejudice*, audience and readers were equally keen to get in out of the wind, and Nora, Avis and Mrs Tate found themselves hard at work once more in the Memorial Hall. Nora wielded the teapot while Avis dealt out buns and cakes with the expertise of a casino croupier, and coins and notes accumulated in the Roses tin.

Seeing all the tables occupied, Mrs Tate was temporarily redundant, so she carried through the last batch of used cups and plates, and prepared to replenish the sausage rolls and buns from her backup box.

The hall seethed with warmth and appreciation, and snatches of conversation floated over the general buzz.

"Nice cuppa. I was ready for that."

"Good little play, wasn't it. Hilary always takes her part well. But it was awful cold for standing about."

"Shocking, isn't it, for June. But it's dry. Has Bert got his hay yet?"

There was a shriek from the kitchen, and the contented chatter froze and scones crumbled in unnerved fingers, as it rose into the battle cry of an outraged cook-

and-bottlewasher. Mrs Tate had taken the lid off her box of sausage rolls and buns.

16 :: Loosing the Pack

Sergeant Postlethwaite saw Aggie Tate coming. Her determined manner caused the less focused stall browsers to part before her, and this convinced him that she was looking for him. It was not an unreasonable deduction, since almost every time he encountered Aggie she was en route to make a complaint about something and the police station was her first port of call. But Sergeant Postlethwaite had had a busy day and it wasn't by any means over, so he didn't intend to go back to the station and spend half an hour making trivial notes for the benefit of Miss Tate's offended sense of decorum. He dodged away from her round the corner and was brought up short by the tweedy bulk of Nora Forthright.

"Afternoon, Perce," she said, without troubling to ask why he was behaving like a schoolboy. "Hasta seen owt of our Wayne?"

"Now then Nora. What kind of a question is that?" He straightened up and resumed his dignity. "I've seen the world and his wife today, and most of 'em in costume. How's he dressed?" But seeing her determined face, he added, "And what's he done?"

Nora, for once, seemed to have difficulty with speech. Her piercing voice dropped a decibel as she said, "He's had his face painted, like a big cat – yeller and black stripes. He'll be wearin' a khaki grey hoodie and jeans. An' if I catch him he'll be wearin' my hands around his neck."

Sergeant Postlethwaite, however, noticed a touch of melodrama in this declaration and he thought Nora was struggling not to laugh.

"Come on Nora, me lass, what's the bairn been up to? Must be summat bad to part you from your teapot."

Nora stepped aside into a doorway, while a party of girls in tired costumes and makeup wandered by and turned along the main street.

"Ah don't want to get the lad into serious trouble," she said, still in unusually muted tones. "but Ah couldn't let Mrs Tate think Ah'd let such a thing go without discipline. It seems our Wayne's fell out with yon Zak child – and about time too. He come askin' for me at Memorial Hall around lunch time, an' seein' what he thought were Zak's lunch box, he – well, Perce, he pissed on the sandwiches."

Sergeant Postlethwaite guffawed, then hastily caught his face in his hand to bring it back into line with the uniform. "Nay, Nora, I never thought the little fella had that much devilment in him!"

Her sharp little eyes twinkled at him from behind the mended spectacles. "So tha sees, Perce, Ah need to find him before Zak's mother does."

They shared a moment of silent merriment and then Sergeant Postlethwaite said, "Well, last I saw of young Wayne he was headed for Pullet St Mary."

"By t'road or fields?" asked Nora.

"Nay, I wouldn't know. Him and young Tom Spencer looked to be having a race. Fair enjoying themselves they were, and gone in a flash."

"How long since?"

Aggie Tate came round the corner. "Oh, there you are, Sergeant! I need to have a little word with you."

"Half an hour maybe," he said to Nora.

"Indeed not," snapped Aggie. "But it is confidential." She looked Nora up and down as though willing her to leave her alone with the Sergeant.

"Now Aggie," he said pacifically, "can't you see I'm busy? I'm sure your trouble will wait."

"Well, mine won't," said Nora, resuming her normal voice. "Thank you for your time, Perce, Ah'll be on me way. See you later, Aggie."

She stumped away round the corner and down the main street, and Aggie, backing the reluctant Sergeant Postlethwaite towards the doorway, began to pour out her doubts and suspicions about the very much less than Honourable Meriel Appleby-Station.

Nora was able to drive a nearly-straight path through the Festival stalls. By now, mothers were starting to resist their children's wheedling for yet another pound, and were drifting past the stalls with no other aim than to get home and off their feet. A different crowd would replace them as the long day faded, the parents with older children ready to spend the evening eating hot dogs and burgers and dancing on the cobbles to the sound of local boy-bands; but for now, the imminent changeover eased Nora's way through the little grey town. As she passed the Memorial Hall she met Richard Station, looking at his watch in a puzzled, dissatisfied way

"Now then Mr S, ye look as though ye lost a shillin' and found sixpence."

"I – well, perhaps you can help, Mrs Forthright. I arranged to meet my wife here when the play was over, but she seems to have vanished. Have you come across her in your travels?"

"Is she in't Hall perhaps?" Nora's concern was genuine, but not very serious. "Havin' a cup of tea?"

"Well no, that's the strange thing. Nobody has seen her at all."

Nora found this incomprehensible. Nobody was ever unobserved in Dangleby.

He went on, "She hasn't called me, and when I call her, the phone rings but it isn't answered. I must admit, Mrs Forthright, I am beginning to be worried about Meriel."

Nora privately agreed that there was a lot to worry about in the Honourable Mrs Appleby-Station. But she had other things to attend to, so she said, "Well, if nobody's sin 'er, yer best road 'ud be to talk to t'police. Perce Postlethwaite's up yon end o't street if ye need him."

Richard looked yet again at his watch. "It's been an hour...I think you're right, Mrs Forthright. Thank you, I'll go and see if I can find him."

***

Alan was not having a good day. Jezza had snatched Meriel's mobile phone out of her pocket the first time it rang, and thrown it into the vacated mummy case, where it bounced along with her handbag, Jezza's wig, and an unwinding spare roll of bandages. The pram, on three wheels, was being difficult.

Meriel, however, was walking blindfold in Alan's grip. She was not being difficult; rather the reverse.

"Such fun," she mumbled. The plaster over her mouth cramped her style but she made the best of it. "Like Blind Man's Buff and Hide and Seek at the same time." Alan's hand on her wrist was hot, sinewy and dry. She leaned towards him, so as he and Rebecca steered her along the thickest parts of the hedges she was as wayward as a supermarket trolley. Alan didn't look back at Jezza's struggles with the pram. He led the way across the mown hay to the gate, then up the rutted gravel track and into the barn.

Alan let go of Meriel and pulled the door almost shut, until only a slice of sunshine lit the dusty interior, but Jezza belted it open again and exploded, dragging the pram in and hurling it off its wheels so that the sawn top and bottom halves of the mummy case cracked against the cow stalls and fell apart. He kicked them, yelled, clutched his toes, and fell over.

"Feckin' dummy! Feckin' sandals!" Jezza got up, still raging, and slammed the door shut. Meriel flinched inside her woollen hat.

"Oh shut up," said Rebecca. "If you'd looked where you were going we'd still have four wheels on the pram."

"Yeah – like it wasn't a feckin' stupid idea from the start."

"It got us out of Dangleby," said Alan. "Phase one is complete. Where's the target's mobile phone?"

"I'm not feckin' lookin' for it."

"Oh for heaven's sake." Rebecca let go of Meriel to search, unsuccessfully, among the wreckage of the mummy case. "Where did you put it?"

"It was in my jacket," mumbled Meriel from behind her plaster.

"I bet you just chucked it in the case," said Alan to Jezza.

"I was hanging' onto your feckin' dummy and pushin' the pram, wasn't I? You might have noticed these costumes aren't big on pockets. Feckin' phone could be anywhere between here an' Dangleby."

"Oh dear," mumbled Meriel.

"Plan B. Bex – we'll use yours."

"On your bike! You're not sending any ransom messages on mine! They'll trace them straight to me. We should've bought a cheap one that we could dump."

"Well, we didn't."

"So that leaves us with Jezza's," said Rebecca.

"Yeah? There's no credit on it. Unless you want to talk to the Bill via 999, you'll have to use yours."

Meriel waited obediently in the cow stalls. She had been hoping to have the woolly hat and the bandages removed. When that happened there should be lighted candles, a cheery fire, deep rugs and cushions and perhaps the offer of a scented bath. However, over the fresh adhesive of her gag her nostrils picked up smells of musty hay, dung, earth floor, wood and stone walls, and they weren't at all what she had been expecting. She turned towards the place where she thought Alan might be, but she heard him walking away.

He went into the hay-mew where he dragged his phone out of his rucksack, and as he came back little beeps announced that he was composing a text message.

"Number?" he said, looking at Rebecca.

"What?"

"I need to send this to Richard Station's mobile number."

"You didn't save it to your phone?"

"Plan A was that we'd get it off hers, remember? The one that's somewhere between here and Dangleby."

They looked at each other. Meriel, completely confused, mumbled through her plaster, "Darlings, why do you want to call Richard?"

Rebecca said, "She'll know his number. We're going to have to take off the gag."

Meriel squeaked as Jezza reached over and ripped it off. "Keep your voice down, lady, and don't try to see us. What's your old fella's number?"

Meriel said, "Alan! Alan? Where are you? My dear, did you have to go to such lengths? And who are...'

"You don't need to know that," said Alan. "C'mon, what's your husband's number?"

Meriel wanted to gesture with her hands, but the bandages held firm. This was really the only thing that inconvenienced her, now that her mouth was free. Being kept in the dark and told very little was so familiar that she felt she could cope.

"Oh dear, you'll think me so stupid, but I don't know his number, I mean I haven't memorised it."

"Yeah right. I bet you could remember if I slapped you."

Rebecca snapped at Jezza, "We agreed, this is action has to be non violent!"

"Oh thank you so much," said Meriel. "Your – er – friend is terribly direct. Don't you think mobile numbers are most awfully difficult? Richard's number is saved on my phone," she added helpfully.

"Yeah, but we haven't feckin' got it, have we?"

"Well don't shout, dear, it was you that took it out of my pocket." Her unmoved vagueness, in spite of her tied hands and blindfold, somehow baffled their attempts to take command of the situation.

"Look," said Alan. "I'll send a text to our cell in Yorkshire. She can look up his number and text him from there."

"Oh yes, I'm sure that would be best," said Meriel chirpily. "Or I could give him the message myself, of course."

Jezza and Rebecca looked at one another in disbelief. "Yeah, like we're gonna send you home when we've gone to all this trouble."

Alan said, "Do try to understand. We want him to stop using animals in his research. This is the deal. He's got to stop torturing them, and turn them loose."

Jezza added, "Or he won't get you back."

17 :: The Hunt

Nora stumped along the narrow pavement of the road to Pullet St Mary, having decided that she would probably get a better view across the fields from there than she would between the hedges of the footpath, but there was no sign of the two boys. Though her pursuit of Wayne had to be carried through, it was now only from a sense of duty, and a simple enjoyment of the day was taking over. She warmed to the activity, and unbuttoned her coat.

She observed a big International tractor mowing steadily round the field to her left, and paused at the gateway to see who might be driving, since it was quite likely to be Jonty, who would certainly have recognised his son if he'd passed this way.

The International lifted its mowing machine as it neared the gate, and Jonty leaned out of the open door. It was strange to see Nora on this route without her shopping bag, so he called, "Is summat up, Ma?"

Nora advanced over the juicy-smelling swathes of cut grass and leaned a hand on the International's massive rear wheel. Her voice easily cut through the noise of the mower drums slowing.

"Hasta seen anyone on't footpath this afternoon?"

"Aye. Aye, there's been a few folk up and down t'footpath today." Jonty pointed across the road to the barn. 'Some I didn't much like t'look of, but ye can't say owt when it's a carnival. Footpath's free to all."

Nora dismissed this. "What about our Wayne? Has he come this way just now?"

"Aye. I reckon he's up in yon field-house at top o' Paradise – him an' that coloured lad. Why, what's he done?"

Nora repeated the lunch-box story, more easily this time. Jonty bowed over the steering wheel and laughed. "La'al bugger. Mind, if that means he's not trailing round wi' Zak any more, I'll be glad."

"Aye. Will the lads be all right playin' in yon buildin'? Is there owt in there to spoil?"

"Nay, they'll be right enough. We cleared it out last week ready for the hay. We'll bale Paradise this afternoon – when I've finished cutting this lot – and Bert might want to lead bales into t'field house tonight, but the lads can't do any harm in there for now."

"Ah'll smack his head anyway," said Nora, her sense of duty reasserting itself. "Ah'll fetch him yam an' Ah'll feed him for ye. Ye'll be late tonight, Ah take it."

"Aye, very likely, but it's all money. Thanks, Ma."

He saluted her with a raised hand, and put the International into gear once more. Nora stayed to observe his mowing; but with a little grunt she acknowledged his skill. "Joss did a good job teachin' our lad," she thought, then she turned away, crossed the road and followed the walls and hedges round the mown fields, on her way to Paradise.

***

Mrs Spencer's mobile had whistled during the choral concert, which meant that she had a text message, but she turned it off so as not to disturb the rest of the audience. She didn't turn it back on till the performance ended, and by that time there were two messages from Tom. One said, "MUM MRS STATION TIED UP IN BARN PLS CALL

999'; the second, sent a minute later, said, "BARN IS PARADISE NR P ST M PLS CALL 999."

She studied these for some minutes. Then she left the Hall and looked up and down the street for one of Sergeant Postlethwaite's constables.

***

Sergeant Postlethwaite was ruminating. He was entertained by Nora's enquiry after Wayne and knew she was perfectly capable of disciplining her grandson. Her story certainly made more sense than Aggie Tate's wofflings over Mrs Station. However, now that Richard Station had reported Meriel's disappearance, the Sergeant had begun to wonder whether Aggie had for once seen something of value. He walked the length of the main street in search of her, questioning various people as he went as to what they knew of the three half-naked Egyptians. He gleaned details about their height, about the mummy made of plaster of Paris bandages, about the pram. He noted the probability that they were two males and a female, and the certainty that they were young and slim built, but nobody had seen them without their wigs and masks, and nobody had seen them after *Price and Prejudice* had ended. It looked as though Aggie might have truly spotted the wolf.

He walked round to her house and found her seated at the dining room table, with pen in hand, no doubt concocting one of her letters to the *Messenger*. Well, if Mr Station's concern was founded on fact, the last thing he'd want was one of Aggie's silly letters being published – and he knew Aggie well enough to be sure that even if he told her not to send it and she agreed, she would change her mind half an hour after he had left. He should probably have a quiet word with Hilary Tiverton-Dick.

"Afternoon Aggie," he said. "I've just been talking to Richard Station."

"It wasn't me," said Aggie. She pushed the pen and writing pad down the back of her chair, and clasped her hands in her lap, a faint flush on her thin cheeks.

He had no idea what she meant, but he assured her, "It's all right, Aggie. Nobody said it was. I'd just like a clearer picture of what you saw in the Square while Mrs Station was watching the play." He moved the black cat off the seat of the chair opposite her, and sat down. Sergeant Postlethwaite had meant this reduction in his height to be friendly, but he suddenly seemed very close to Aggie, and she shrank back an inch or two. The cat took a position on the hearthrug and licked itself in an offended way.

He brought out his all weather notebook, and a pencil. "Come on, Aggie, what can you tell me?"

"Well, I saw her go off with those three actors. Drama students. The ones with the mops on their heads."

"Now, think carefully, Aggie. Did you actually see her go? Which way?"

"Well, no, I didn't actually SEE her go, but she must have gone down the alley."

"Why do you think that? Had you been watching her?"

Aggie writhed. She had learned that afternoon that Sergeant Postlethwaite had a low opinion of her – in the heat of battle, Mrs Tate had reported him calling her a 'snooping spinster' and the blister of that still hurt – so she longed to be able to say something of consequence. She was not certain what would convince him, the truth or her embroidered version. The crackle of the radio on his shoulder unnerved her enough to make her choose the truth.

"I was watching the play, through the café window. Richard – Mr Station – was reading his part. When it was someone else's turn I looked away and I noticed her by the lamp standard. The one with the tub of blue flowers."

"Surfinias?" suggested Sergeant Postlethwaite, making a note.

Aggie, still partly dazzled by the memory of Richard Station in the play, wondered if "Sir Phineas" might be a character, and maintained a considering silence. The Sergeant coughed, and asked, "Could you have missed her going? Do you think she might have gone another way, like across the Square?"

"I have a very keen eye, Sergeant," said Aggie, recovering. "And other people would have seen her, wouldn't they? You wouldn't be here if they had."

He moved on. "Is that when you saw these – er – Egyptians? When she was standing by the flowers?"

"Yes, they were in the alley behind her. With their trolley. And when I looked they were gone and so was she. So she must have gone off with them, mustn't she?"

Sergeant Postlethwaite didn't contradict her. "Did you get any impression as to what they were doing? Were they watching the play?"

"Oh no," said Aggie with certainty, "they were watching her."

His radio crackled and a voice called for him.

"Excuse me," he said to Aggie, and bent his head to the radio. "Thank you. No, it isn't a hoax. We need to get onto it right away. Ask for a patrol car. I'm on my way now." He closed his notebook and stood up. "Now, Aggie, I don't want you making a big fuss over this with the newspaper." He cocked an eyebrow towards the hiding place of her pen and writing pad. "Mrs Station has almost certainly been kidnapped, and you must keep your very valuable evidence confidential for the moment."

Aggie sat primly straight. "Naturally, Sergeant. My lips are sealed." Her expression brimmed with self-importance.

"We don't want to put Mrs Station in any more danger than we can help. Thank you for your time."

18 :: In at the Kill

Alan, Rebecca and Jezza went from the cow stalls through the latched door into the hay-mew, a wide, dim, windowless two-storey space that Jonty and Bert had cleared for the crop now drying on Paradise. Piled against the wall were their clothes and bags and a jar of cleansing cream (certified not tested on animals). Their shaven heads gleamed in the half light as they removed their makeup. Meriel, still hooded and pinioned, could not see where they had gone, and remained patiently standing in the middle of the cow stalls. Hearing the rattle as they threw their masks and wigs into the mummy case she called, "Do you think I might sit down?"

"Yeah," said Jezza, who was stripping off his costume, "just fold your knees and sit right there."

"Oh but I can't do that, you see my arms have...'

Rebecca marched back to her, took her by the elbows and pushed her to one of the cow stalls, where Jonty and Bert had stacked the remaining few bales of last year's hay. "Sit there," she said, and Meriel collapsed onto them, protesting faintly as the stalks prickled her legs.

Jezza pulled on his street clothes. "Yeah well, I'm off," he said, and went back to untangle his bike from the other two in the second cow-stall.

"And where d'you think you're going?" said Alan.

"To get something to eat. I could murder a chicken jalfrezi."

"Jezza!" cried Rebecca. "What about our principles?"

"I've been perished all day and I'm not going to munch on veg-and-two-veg just for a feckin' principle."

Meriel sighed, "Oh, I'm afraid I can't possibly eat curry."

"I'm not getting it for you, you droopy cow."

Alan, wiping the last of the makeup from round his eyes, said firmly, "Jez. You'll stock up for all of us and bring it back here. Make sure it's vegan."

"Yeah right boss, and who's going to pay?"

Alan looked at Rebecca. She shrugged and ignored him so he reached for his jeans and dragged out a twenty pound note. Jezza pocketed it, swung a leg over the bike, tried to open the door, threw down the bike, opened the door, and finally wobbled away down the field.

Rebecca shut the door behind him and asked, "And exactly how long do you plan to hold her here?"

"As long as it takes."

Meriel, who had now managed to rearrange herself, said, "But if you'll just untie my arms I could be ready any time, dear."

Rebecca looked from Meriel to Alan and her eyebrows lifted dangerously.

He held up his hands. "Whoa now, back off. Don't get ideas."

"Why does she keep calling you dear?"

"She calls everybody dear."

"Not the way she calls *you* dear," snapped Rebecca. She bundled up her costume and shoved it at him. "Is that why you've kept on about working from the inside? All that cosy time alone together."

"Bex, I don't have any designs on the woman." He stood clutching the costume to his chest, and Meriel gave a little moan of disappointment.

"I don't believe you," said Rebecca, picking up her jeans and viciously shaking the hay off them. "I want her safely tied up at Nether Gusset, where I can keep an eye on her. And I don't want to spend any more time here. There are bound to be rats. Let's get her away as soon as possible."

"Agreed, but we don't want to be seen. We have to wait until the Festival is over and everyone's gone home. We discussed all this."

"No, you *told* us about it, and pretty sketchy it was too. You still haven't worked out a plan to get us away, have you?"

"I did, but you were the one who vetoed stealing a car."

They went on bickering as they struggled into their clothes. Above them, in the first-floor hayloft, Wayne's cheetah-striped face looked over the edge at them, then stealthily retreated.

***

Nora stepped prudently out of Jezza's way as he wobbled down the field. He didn't see her until the last minute, and then he swore at her and wobbled out onto the road, where he stood on the pedals and raced off, and she lost sight of him. She didn't know who he was, but she had noticed the shaven head and the greasy, discoloured face, and heard him swearing. You never knew what people like that might get up to: smoking and drugs and stuff. She thought she might suggest that Bert and Jonty should lock up the barn once the hay was in. If the hay caught fire, they might lose the roof as well as the crop.

She chewed over Jezza's swear-words. They didn't mean much to her, but the irritation heightened her avenging mood as she stumped along, her stout shoes crunching over the gravel, towards the barn.

Like many Cumbrian 'field houses' the barn butted into the slope, and the track wound round the back up an earth ramp to a double door at first floor level. This was where Bert and Jonty would deliver their trailer loads of new hay later in the evening. The front door was only used in winter, to let cattle in and out of the stalls to drink at the water trough. Nora thought that Wayne and Tom would have found the upper level much more attractive than the stalls, which tended to smell of cow-muck even in summer, so she was expecting to hear boys' feet thundering over the bare wooden floor. Instead she heard arguing voices inside. Not Wayne or Tom, but a young man and a girl. She couldn't make out what they were saying. "Time Ah gave in and asked about hearin' aids," she thought. She pushed the door wide open and the afternoon sunlight fell across Meriel, blind under the woolly hat, quietly weeping.

Nora took in the scene at one glance, including the awkward pose that suggested tied hands. She twitched off the woolly hat immediately, but Meriel's eyes were still adjusted to darkness, so in the blaze of sunshine Nora's bulky silhouette and flapping coat might have been either friend or foe.

She sniffled, and hiccupped. "Who is that?"

"It's me, Nora Forthright." Investigation could wait. She reached into her cardigan for her Swiss Army knife to cut the ties, and remembered as she did so that the knife was in Wayne's pocket, not her own. "Stay there a minnit, Mrs Station." Hands on hips, she shouted at the beamed ceiling, "Wayne! Are ye up there?"

The piercing enquiry did not bring Wayne, but Alan, who threw open the door from the sink-mew.

"Oh, it's thee, Alan," said Nora. She'd seen him so often working in the garden for Meriel that she didn't even think to ask him why he was there, though the shaven head was a bit of a shock. "Hasta seen our Wayne?"

For Alan this was disaster. The target was sitting there, no longer hooded, but staring at him. Of course she was still tied up, but the nosy old bat beside her would know all the details of their hideout and she'd have no trouble identifying him to the police.

He discounted Meriel. Nora was the one who must be silenced. Well, they had managed Meriel quite easily and he did not imagine Nora would be much different, so he threw himself into the attack.

Nora, although surprised, was a veteran of the farm who had many times dealt successfully with larger animals than Alan. She merely sidestepped a trifle, and drove one stout shoe down on his sandalled toes. Then as he fell she brought her forearm up under his chin, and with a moan he folded into the floor.

By now she was roused to battle status, so when Rebecca opened the door of the mew the moment of hesitation was a gift. Nora walked into her with an outstretched palm, like a rugby player fending off a tackle. The slight body collapsed backwards, and Nora slammed the door shut. In the cow stalls, Alan was trying to drag his face out of the dirt, but she stumped over to him and without much effort (or bending her knees) leaned down and twisted his arm up his back. She put one foot on it to keep it there. She considered standing on him, but it had been a long day, and her legs were too tired.

"Wayne!" she commanded, pushing her glasses back up her nose with her free hand. "Ah know yer up there! Come down!"

Two boys dropped like cats from the first floor into the hay-mew and landed on top of Rebecca, and with that, the rescue of the Honourable Meriel Appleby-Station was more or less complete.

19 :: Aftermath

Reinforcements arrived in a very short space of time, when Sergeant Postlethwaite and his constables bounced up the track in a patrol car. They jumped out and ran into the barn, and without discussion they dragged Alan out from under Nora and handcuffed him.

"See if there's anyone else," said Sergeant Postlethwaite.

"In yonder," said Nora, and seeing that the constables had Alan secure, she pulled open the door of the mew where Wayne and Tom were gleefully sitting on Rebecca, who was face down on the hay-cushioned floor alternately sneezing and swearing.

The constables handcuffed her and pulled her to her feet. She squealed at Alan, "That was pathetic! Being beaten by – by an old woman!"

Alan retorted, "Not as pathetic as being held down by two school kids."

Wayne and Tom brushed the hay off their clothes, laughed and punched each other's arms, and followed the constables out of the mew.

Nora favoured them all with an ironic grin.

"Ah used to could wrestle a bullock, so yon wasn't much of a contest." While Sergeant Postlethwaite took the names of their suspects and went through other formalities, she reclaimed her Swiss Army knife from Wayne and cut Meriel's bandages from her wrists. "There now, Mrs Station."

"Appleby-Station," whispered Meriel, drawing her arms painfully from behind her back. "It's the one thing..."

"Yes, yes, Ah know. Are ye all right?"

"Yes, I think so." She turned on Alan. "You've disappointed me! I always treated you as a friend, and now this!"

He tried to achieve a stern, proud expression, but only succeeded in looking sullen. Meriel pulled a hankie from her jacket pocket and miserably blew her nose, while Sergeant Postlethwaite finished cautioning Alan and Rebecca, and spoke into his radio to announce their arrest.

"There's another one, you know," quavered Meriel. "He went to get something to eat."

"Don't worry, Mrs Station, we'll catch up with him." He spoke into his radio again and the two constables pushed Alan and Rebecca towards the door.

But Meriel called out, "I just want to know why – please could you wait? Alan, my dear, why did you do this? I thought you were fond of me."

Nora raised her eyebrows at the note of disappointment.

Rebecca screamed at Alan, "You see! I told you!"

Alan ignored her and shouted at Meriel. "We were protesting against the work your husband is doing on animals!"

"My HUSBAND?" said Meriel.

Sergeant Postlethwaite brought out his notebook. "Hang about, lads," he said to the constables. "Let's get this down while it's hot." He reminded Alan, "You've been cautioned."

"We don't care about that. We're nothing."

"Are you ready to make a statement?"

"Yes, a statement about the use of animals in research."

"Cruelty in the name of science," said Rebecca.

"I shan't be recording any of that. If there's nowt else – ' He closed the notebook, and the constables prepared to move their prisoners on.

Meriel said, "Oh, dear. Are you the people who've been painting messages on the windows, and sending us vile letters, and pushing filth through our letterbox?"

"Oh, much more than that!" said Rebecca. "They put a bomb – " She stopped as Alan made a lunge towards her and was grappled back. "OK, OK."

Sergeant Postlethwaite smiled grimly. "We don't care, eh? That would be the package the bomb squad took from under Mr Station's Discovery?" He glanced at Wayne, and then consulted the pages of his notebook. "I hear tell that one or two lads have been trespassing in the garden of The Grange."

Wayne opened his mouth to say, "I never," but Nora's work-hardened hand squeezed his shoulder. He read it correctly as a "Shut up" warning, and subsided.

"Those lads ought to be grateful," said the Sergeant blandly, "that Mr Station declined to press charges. On account of them pulling out suspicious dangling wires and suchlike. Would you have anything to say about that, Miss Bain?"

Rebecca muttered, "No comment."

Wayne grinned and nudged Tom, and the Sergeant's pencil made a full stop.

Meriel, arriving at her conclusion some time after everyone else, said, "You must be the reason we have to live with all those cameras. It's very inconvenient."

"Don't encourage 'em," advised Nora, but she was too late. Alan was off again.

"It's even more inconvenient for the animals! Caged up! Assaulted! That's why we have to get publicity for them."

"It's not *good* publicity, dear," protested Meriel

"Any publicity is good."

"But how does it help them? And I'm sorry if I'm selfish, but I don't see what I have to do with it."

"You stupid cow!" he screamed. "We weren't going to let you go unless Station let his own victims go!"

Sergeant Postlethwaite made a note with great emphasis and satisfaction.

"Richard never kidnapped anybody," said Meriel.

"What about the animals in his labs?" said Rebecca. "They are all victims!"

"He didn't kidnap them," said Meriel stubbornly. "I don't think you can actually *know* what Richard does. I'm *sure* you don't know what animals you were trying to free."

"We don't care. They're all equal. Rabbits, monkeys or goats, they're all the same to us."

Meriel gave a nervous little whinny – the nearest that she could get to being contemptuous. "But my dear, he is educating rats."

Rebecca shrieked, "Rats!"

Alan said coldly, "What do you mean, educating them?"

"Well, yes, rats. He trains them to do constipated tasks. It's part of his research into Alzheimer's disease. Or do I mean Parkinson's? Anyway, it's to do with helping people, do you see?"

"That doesn't alter the fact that the rats are slaves, being tortured without consent – prisoners who must suffer, because they can't protest."

Nora had had enough. "Perce! Are we gonna stand here all day, or am I gonna tek these bairns away yam?"

Sergeant Postlethwaite, feeling that the prisoners had sufficiently incriminated themselves, pocketed his notebook with unruffled dignity. He turned to Meriel and said, "We'll send a car along, Mrs Station, to bring you to the, er, station. We'll need you to make a statement. Will you be all right until then?"

Meriel sat down sadly on the hay bale. This wasn't how she'd seen the day ending. "I suppose so."

"That's fine. Mr Station and young Thomas's Mum are there already. I think Mrs Forthright might stay with you till the car comes. Will you do that, Nora?"

"Ah will," she said. "Ah'll be glad of a sit down here out o't wind. These two lads have a story to tell about how they come to be here in t'fust place. That'll entertain us just grand."

Nora waited till the police had set off before she seized the boys in a tweedy hug.

"Now then, lads, ye did a right good job. I reckon there's summat fishy at bottom of it but I'll not ask, seein' it turned out all right."

"So brave!" said Meriel, with a fluttering attempt at a smile.

"Tell yer tale straight to t'Sergeant and I shall be fair proud of ye."

Tom and Wayne wriggled out of Nora's grasp, united in distrust of this soft behaviour. She at once righted matters – as she had intended since heading out of Dangleby Memorial Hall – by giving Wayne a cuff over the head.

"And *that* is for shamin' me by pissin' in the sandwiches."

20 :: The Messenger

Wayne sat on the grassy bank of the field house at Paradise, surrounded by the delicious smell of the hay stacked inside. It was the Saturday after the Festival and he was waiting for Tom. He could see him in the distance, dribbling a football along the footpath from Pullet St Mary towards their rendezvous. His Dad had got permission from Bert Askew, and the boys had arranged by phone message and text to meet on the new green aftermath of the field. When Tom got a bit nearer, he booted the football towards Wayne, and did a kind of running war dance after it. Wayne saw that he had a bow in one hand and a clutch of arrows in the other.

"Did you bring yours?"

"Course I did!" said Wayne, waving the weapons back at him.

"Race you to the ramp!"

Wayne gave a derisive yell, but a sense of fairness made him wait till Tom came level before he sprinted towards the field house. He hit the ramp door two yards ahead, whereupon Tom arrived and knocked him flat.

"Mind me arrows!"

"Oops, sorry."

They picked themselves up, then the bows and arrows, and sat in the sunshine to compare their handiwork.

Tom looked over the arrows Wayne had made from long summer shoots of sycamore. "I tried making a bow out of that stuff, but it just bends and snaps."

"Your bow's ash," said Wayne. Playing Spiderman had made him familiar with the saplings that grew up around his favourite trees.

"All right, I know that! There's an old tree in the garden, and this one grew back after it was cut down. My Dad sawed it off for me."

Wayne said, "My Dad said hazel might be good. He trimmed it and he got me that string too, cos the stuff I bought was crap."

He felt shy about capping everything Tom said, but it was true; once the hay was in, his Dad had had time to help him.

"Can I have a go with it?" asked Tom.

"All right." He exchanged the glossy spotted hazel for the grey ash.

They ran about shooting and missing, picking up the arrows, and shooting again, making their fingers sore on the strings. They shot at wisps of dry grass, at feathers, at bits of paper blown from the Festival. It didn't really matter that the flights stripped one by one from the sycamore shafts, or that Tom's ash and Wayne's hazel first acquired a permanent bend, and then snapped.

"Maybe we could ask for proper bows for our birthdays," said Tom.

They had learned enough for the moment and were ready to stop. They drifted back to the field house, where they sat on the grass, taking the strings off the broken bows. Wayne changed his grip on the biggest piece and began to dig in the turf. Tom didn't stop him, just sat with his arms round his knees and watched.

When Wayne had worked his way down to the stone that made up the bank, he glanced at Tom and said shyly, "You were really brave on Sat'd'y."

"Oh!" said Tom. "Well, yeah. Thanks."

"Even if it was only a girl that you tackled."

Tom's laugh was as big as his mother's. "I've got to be brave to play football with you!"

Wayne launched himself at Tom with a yell and the two boys rolled down the slope, punching one another. When they'd worked off their embarrassment they collected the football, and started passing it to each other.

Tom asked, "Why haven't they picked you to play yet? You're fast."

"Mr Benson talks about teamwork. He says I just get the ball and run for goal." Wayne pulled a face. "I dunno why that's wrong, except you or somebody else'll take it off me and that's all I ever see of it."

"Duh! That's why we practise passing. Didn't you realise? Look." Tom fetched his broken bow and stuck it upright in the dry soil. "That's a defender, right? Well if you just run at him, he'll prob'ly tackle you. But if you pass the ball to me, you can sprint round him and I'll pass the ball back to you. See? Go on, do it!"

He did it. They practised over and over until they could run the whole length of Paradise, co-operating like hunting lions.

***

Nora Forthright pulled her front door shut and stumped off down the lane towards the Post Office. The weather was warm enough for her to have put away the tweed coat, but her feet were still stoutly shod and she still carried the faded canvas bag.

The bell tinkled as she strode into the shop, and Aggie Tate, who was on her way out, simpered at her and offered congratulations on the rescue of Meriel.

“Although I did have a *good deal* to do with it myself,” she whispered. “Sergeant Postlethwaite said my evidence will be most valuable.”

She twitched her nose and shoulders and went out.

“Now then, Mrs Forthright,” said David, giving her full title in acknowledgement of her celebrity status, “to what do we owe the honour of your stalwart presence?”

“Oh do give ower, David,” snapped Nora. “What wi’ newspapers an’ television johnnies Ah’s been fair mithered this last week. Ah’s lookin’ for a present for our Wayne. It’s ’is birthday in a fortnight and I want a good penknife for ’im.”

David groaned a little as he bent down to unlock a glass cabinet, and present a selection of small folding knives. “These are all legal, but you might warn him not to take it to school.”

He hobbled off to serve another customer while she debated. She chose a knife with a bright red casing, and a birthday card. When she paid for them she asked if he ever carried children’s bow and arrow sets.

“No, but I do have a supplier. Safety-tipped only, of course.”

“Order me two sets,” she said. “Ah’ll call again.”

Sergeant Postlethwaite passed her in the doorway. David listened intently in hopes of overhearing more details about the kidnapping, but they only exchanged a few polite words, and he gleaned nothing that the county newspaper hadn’t revealed on Friday. The Sergeant was complaining of arthritis in his writing hand, and asked for aspirins.

David couldn’t stand the suspense any longer. “She’s a grand old girl, our Nora.”

“She is, aye, no doubt about it.”

"Pitching in like that to rescue Mrs Station. I heard she took on three of them single-handed."

"Oh, you shouldn't believe everything you hear," said Sergeant Postlethwaite.

"There *was* one weird tale though, Perce...'

"Go on," said the Sergeant, patiently. "Mind, I can't guarantee to tell you much."

"What's this rumour about a blow-up doll being found at Paradise? Eh? Burst, too, I heard. Sounds a bit racy, even for Bert Askew. What's that all about, eh?"

Sergeant Postlethwaite leaned forward confidentially.

"Blonde hair, and the same size as Mrs Station." He lifted his eyebrows and added with a suggestive cock of the head, "Hm? Lonely barn, middle of nowhere... Think about it."

"Get away," breathed David. "Yer jokin'. And when young Alan was planning all that time to carry her off – do you mean to say...'

"Aye."

"Good God. I didn't think he had it in him."

Sergeant Postlethwaite let out a guffaw of laughter. "What are you imagining, you silly old fool? They wrapped plaster of Paris round Friendly Wendy to make the mummy case. She must have got popped when they cut it to make the lid."

***

Phil and Hilary Tiverton-Dick sat in front of her computer, at the window of the room that functioned as the *Messenger* office. Hilary had acquired several little stories for the next issue, some contributed by the teachers, some by enthusiastic members of the dance troupes and the choirs, others by the Secretaries of the

Scribblers and the dramatic and musical societies; but the rest of the Festival had still to be written-up, by herself. Having set up the advertisement pages she was scrolling through his photographs of the Festival.

They had short-listed some good shots of the Parade and of *Price and Prejudice* as a record of the outdoor events, and were now trying to agree on which ones they should use.

"I'm surprised," said Hilary, "that Sergeant Postlethwaite didn't want many photos of the kidnappers with their chariot thing. You did get some fantastic shots of them."

"Surreal," said Phil, absently, flicking through images of Richard Station reading a script. "We can keep some back for the report when it comes to trial."

"That one of Richard would go well with the piece about the kidnapping. I know he's acting, but he looks so worried."

Phil moved a copy into a folder, and they went on working. After a while she said, "Let's take a break. Coffee?"

When she came back with the mugs, he was opening the morning's post.

"Anything worthwhile?" she asked.

"The usual nonsense. A poem in wonky quatrains, all about the poetry readings. A couple of Letters to the Editor. Mrs Station is getting worked up again. Listen to this:

~ ~

Dear Hilary Timber Deck

I'm at my wits' end. The excitements of last weekend's Festival have left my husband feeling very *low and he has taken to spending all his spare time in the Owl and Wicket. He says he learnt this method of consolation from some GCSE students who were coping with stress by 'going down the pub to celebrate being withdrawn from the exams."*

When he comes home he has nothing intelligent to say and simply goes to bed and snores. I'm dreadfully worried that he will meet someone else while he is out, then the boys will have to leave St Gullible's Prep School and they and I will be left alone. Please help.

Desperately
Hon. Meriel Appleby-Station.

~ ~

Hilary said, 'Any sensible woman would have her husband wrapped round her little finger after all that's happened this week. But no. She has to whinge about him in public. Why doesn't she go to the Owl and Wicket and share the Happy Hour with him?"

He agreed. "I'm sure if she put her mind to it she could see off a dozen rivals."

"Depends what you call a mind," said Hilary, with a grin. "She needs to take lessons from Nora."

"I doubt whether doing the right thing by accident is something Nora could teach. I don't suppose anyone taught her."

"She does her best by sending letters to us, doesn't she?"

"And guess who this other letter's from! I thought she might be on about the animal rights people, but she isn't – you'd think the whole thing had never happened. You remember Reverend what's his name talking on the radio, about supermarket prices being too high because they include the cost of shoplifting?"

"Oh yes. He suggested law-abiding pensioners should be excused for nicking things?"

"Well, here's Nora's take on it."

~~~~~~~~~~~~~~~~~~~~~~~~~~~~~~~~

Now then, Hobnailed

I'm on a pension and so are most of my friends, and we're not so strong as we were. We used-to-could handle all makes of things, four bales of hay at yance, two bullocks and their mother, six DEFRA fellers and a tax inspector. But nowadays with cash being tight I nobbut can practise once a month down the Pullet St Mary road with a ten pound bag of taties and a bag of Self Raising flour.

Now there's yon old vicar feller on the radio telling us we should all be shoplifting. He should be ashamed of his self. How can we start that at our time of life? We wouldn't get the Post Office more than knee high off the ground these days.

Yrs sternly

Nora Forthright

~~~~~~~~~~~~~~~~~~~~~~~~~~~~~~~~

Hilary chuckled. "You know, when the old bat goes upstairs to join Joss, a mighty era will come to a close."

Phil said thoughtfully, "On the other hand, a whole new one might open for Joss!"

"All the more reason to propose a toast, darling – long life to Nora Forthright."

The End – for now

Other books coming shortly from Jackdaw E Books

Dragon Bait

Princess Andra volunteers to act as bait for the dragon ravaging her father's lands, on condition that she is released from an arrangement to marry a foreign prince.

Unfortunately the Knight Rescuer who turns up is not the trusty old retainer she expects, but an unknown conservationist who wants the dragon, not the lady. After that very little goes according to plan.

ISBN 978-0-9573612-1-8

GENRE: Comic fantasy (age 9-12).

Here's a sample:

Last Wednesday

'I'm glad that's all over,' said Princess Andra. 'Being *engaged to a foreign prince* is like saying you'll marry a country. I almost feel sorry for Elisa.'

Her sister had been betrothed that afternoon to Gerald of Terragonia, and the happy pair were following the King and Queen towards the private apartments, Elisa sleek as always in embroidered cream satin, Gerald's slight figure bright in scarlet and gold lace. Andra was trailing some way behind, alongside her fat brother Bertram.

He panted, 'It'll be your turn next.'

Andra snorted. 'You needn't think you'll escape, Jelly-Belly. It's just that they're struggling to find a foreign princess who's as fat as you.'

Before he could reply, their mother's voice rang down the corridor: 'Andra! Bertram! Come into the small drawing room. Your father has something he wants to say to you.'

Bertie looked speculatively at Andra. 'What have you been up to now?'

'Why me?'

'It usually is.'

'Only because you and Elisa can't be bothered.'

At the doorway of the drawing room, the King turned to Prince Gerald.

'Little family matter to discuss,' he said, offering his hand. 'Give us half an hour, eh?'

The Queen added benignly, 'We are sure you'll understand.'

'Oh, of course, wouldn't dweam of buttin' in,' said Gerald. He shook hands with the King, bowed over the Queen's outstretched fingers, and gave Elisa a peck on the cheek before he wandered off towards the visitors' wing of the palace. Elisa smiled in her usual empty-headed way, and Gerald's supporting officers saluted and went after him. At one point it seemed their green uniforms might tramp right over the top of his scarlet, but at the last moment the most senior officer gave an order and they fell back into a slow-march that carried them all efficiently round the corner.

In the drawing room, where the sun struck between satin curtains onto a peacock silk carpet, the King and Queen seated themselves on gilded chairs, and Elisa went to the window and stood looking out. Bertram pulled a book from his pocket, and lay full length on a couch where he began to read. Andra found a cushion, arranged her skirts round her feet and sat down cross-legged. She was wondering whether Gerald's officers ate and slept to attention. It was very odd that the King and Queen of Terragonia had sent soldiers to accompany their son. Why hadn't they come to Stellaria themselves, if only to look at Elisa, sigh and go away?

The Queen said, 'Now! While we are all together, your father has an announcement to make.'

'Cassie, you would do this much better than me.'

She turned her darkest stare full on to him. 'Sebastian, we are relying on you.'

'Er – yes. Right. Well, I've received disturbing news from the City Councillors. You see, while we have been celebrating the betrothal, the Councillors have drawn Elisa's name in their Ballot of Eligible Damsels.'

Andra sat up straighter and her eyes brightened. Ooh, that was sneaky of them. Scream, Elisa, I dare you.

'In view of our celebrations,' said the King, 'I have asked them not to publish anything, but from the time the betrothal ceremony is officially complete –'

'Tomorrow,' said the Queen.

'Elisa has seven days before she must act as Dragon Bait.'

COACHMAN

Queen Victoria is crowned, and England is at peace, but 1838 isn't a good year to be a coachman, not even when you're good looking and ambitious. George Davenport travels to London with his bride Lucy, determined to make the most of his skill in driving a four-in-hand of horses. But industry is hitting its stride, and as railways open across the country they threaten to kill off the work he loves. George finds employment with William Chaplin, the "Napoleon of coaching," and discovers that the boss's daughter has designs on him that have nothing to do with his driving.

ISBN 978-0-9573612-5-6

GENRE: Historical fiction

Here's a sample:

April 1838

"You up there! Wake up."

George heard the voice, but his eyelids refused to lift. Surely he could doze for a few minutes while the coach changed horses? Now that the roof-top seat was still, oblivion was sucking him into its delicious depths, so that he was back in Carlisle with Lucy, saying goodbye in the firelight, wrapping her in his arms while dawn filtered through the shutters.

In his half-dream she was repeating, "Go...I'll follow you as soon as I'm better. Go now. Go." And he didn't want to, but he'd applied for the job and if he didn't keep the appointment ...

The voice spoke again at his elbow: "Coachman!"

The title roused him, but then he remembered he wasn't the driver, only a very weary passenger on the "Albion," who'd travelled all yesterday and half today. And he'd left Lucy behind at the Blue Bell. Damn it, he should never have set off without her. He should have waited till she was well...

"Come on, boy. Are you fit to drive us?"

He dragged himself out of sleep, and saw the grey-bearded guard balanced nonchalantly on the tread, half way up the coach side, waiting for him to answer.

His driving whip had slipped towards the passenger next to him. He retrieved it, and adjusted his hat against the spring sunshine.

"Where are we?" His lips and tongue were clumsy with tiredness.

"Stony Stratford, the Cock Hotel. Look, I need a coachman. I've told 'im 'e mustn't drive but 'e will, unless I put someone on the box pretty quick."

George struggled to understand. Down in front of the coach, a team fretted at the restraining hands of the ostlers.

"He's never been this bad afore," said the guard. "The Guv'nor will dismiss the both of us if I let 'im drive – and if I don't, *I'll* have to drive, and then we won't get up to Town this side of dark. Then I see'd your whip and I thought, ah, there's a coachman, so maybe we're in luck."

The body of the coach shuddered. Something very heavy must be loading, to disturb its massive springs. A hat, a head and shoulders came up, fell back, and reappeared. They were followed by a body wrapped in a greatcoat, a body that chuckled and rolled as the stable men pushed it upwards, that heaved itself belly-first onto the driving-seat amid a gust of brandy fumes, and then lost its hat. George woke up fully, all his driving experience shouting outrage.

"He isn't going to drive, is he? That barrel of lard! He's paralytic."

A bonnet poked out of the window below and screeched, "Coachman! We are five minutes behind time! Be pleased to start!"

The driver roared back, "Immee-jusly, Madame! Throw me the reins, boys, tally-ho." He accepted his hat from a stablehand and placed it on his head with a royal disregard for its orientation.

"I'll have the devil's own job to get him off the box now," sighed the guard. "Hurry up, climb forrard, or he'll drive us all to Kingdom Come."

"I think I'd better," said George, and the guard slapped his arm encouragingly and jumped down.

JACKDAW E BOOKS
Daw Bank, Greenholme, Tebay, Penrith, Cumbria
CA10 3TA
England

http://www.jackdawebooks.co.uk

Lightning Source UK Ltd.
Milton Keynes UK
UKOW052345111112

202050UK00001B/1/P